THE MYSTERIOUS WU FANG:
THE CASE OF THE HIDDEN SCOURGE

THE CASE OF
THE HIDDEN SCOURGE

By Robert J. Hogan

ALTUS PRESS • 2017

CHAPTER 1
THE CRIME LORD SPEAKS

THIRTY FEET below the teeming, cosmopolitan city of Singapore, strange things were taking place. There were rooms down there, large, comfortable, well-furnished rooms with vaulted ceilings that had been hewn out of solid rock many years before. They served now as a hideout for Wu Fang, the fiendish yellow Dragon Lord of Crime and Emperor of Death, who had very recently escaped death himself.

In the center of the largest underground room stood an operating table upon which rested a glass object resembling a sarcophagus. Thick, springy carpets of powder blue and gold covered the floor. Thick drapes covered the four walls and ceiling, concealing all means of entrance and exit.

A group of people were gathered in the room. Some could be called humans but others would scarcely answer to that description. There were brown-skinned Malayans—half-naked beasts, clothed only in loin cloths. They had muscular bodies and horrible, brutal faces.

The Chinese present seemed to be divided into two classes. Some of them looked as brutal and disreputable as any of the Malayan natives, but the rest were well-dressed and apparently quite intelligent.

Then there were representatives of other nations. One debonair fellow looked strikingly French; another was a typical

1

Wu Fang stepped menacingly
through the panel.

Englishman. Two medium-built men were distinctly an American and a Spaniard respectively. All these Occidentals were neatly dressed and suave-looking, but upon close examination, one would have felt instinctively that they were devilishly clever and ruthless.

Several girls were included in the group. All of them were beautiful, but two of them—a tall, blonde, blue-eyed young woman and a pretty, innocent-appearing little Chinese girl—stood out most prominently. The latter did not look to be more than twelve, but she was in reality quite a few years older and as ruthless and cunning as any of the male agents.

These, then, were the agents of Wu Fang, servants who would do his bidding regardless of the consequences. As they huddled around the operating table, the very air itself was tinged with tense expectancy and anticipation. They seemed to be awaiting something that was of the utmost importance to all of them.

All eyes were turned upon that glass object in the center of the room through which they could see the figure of a long, gaunt Chinaman lying face up.

To all appearances, Wu Fang was dead. No sign of life was visible within that glass sarcophagus. From the side of the room nearest the head of the glass case, two rubber tubes extended under the bottom of the operating table and vanished under the glass hood.

Every figure in the room tensed suddenly as the sound of a gong, deep, hollow, but far away, came to them. Then all eyes shifted from the still form of Wu Fang under the glass case to a corner of the room where two drapes were parting.

A little Chinaman dressed in the white garb of a hospital surgeon quickly stepped inside. His olive eyes flashed about the room, took in every face in one sharp glance. He had taken only one step into the room when he stopped and spoke in a quick, jerky, high-pitched voice.

"I will tell you why you have been called here," he said. "While I perform the operation of lifting the glass hood, thereby terminating the secret treatment of our master, Wu Fang, you are to remain perfectly motionless. You are not even to breathe. You must keep your eyes on Wu Fang constantly, and with your brain, you will believe that he must be restored. Do I make myself clear?"

Heads bowed silently and raised again in assent.

"Very well," the little Chinese doctor continued. "We are ready."

He stepped quickly to the center of the room beside the glass covered operating table and raised his right hand to the ceiling drapes. He spoke a few short words in rapid Chinese.

"Now I am ready," he said.

The agents of Wu Fang who were assembled in the underground chamber stiffened and stood like statues, their eyes glued upon the face of Wu Fang. The glass cover was rising slowly as though by some mysterious force. It went higher and higher until it finally vanished into the drapes above.

The little white-garbed Chinese doctor bent over Wu Fang. His eyes blazed for a moment with a queer look as he stretched out his right hand and moved it slowly forward and backward a few inches above the face of the Dragon Lord of Crime.

With his left hand, the doctor brought out a tiny instrument that couldn't be seen plainly by the other agents. He placed it with a quick, professional little jab in the temple of the yellow fiend and held it there for a moment. Then he drew away from Wu Fang and stood back, waiting. Again his eyes blazed as though fires were kindled in them.

There was a sudden stir as every agent in that room gasped in astonishment. Their master, Wu Fang, was moving! His eye lids were parted and his eye balls rolled back and forth. Next, his head turned from side to side. They could see a slight scar on his head, just above the temple, where the hair had not yet grown long enough to cover his recent wound.

Now the yellow fiend was raising his head and moving his hands and arms. He looked about the room, slightly puzzled.

Quickly, the little Chinese doctor stepped up to the side of the operating table and taking hold of the thin, gaunt arms, helped the Emperor of Death to a sitting posture.

Wu Fang's green eyes met those of the Chinese doctor and the yellow fiend smiled triumphantly.

"It was a success, Doctor Wong," he said. "Wu Fang was right."

"Yes, Master," the doctor nodded. "As always, you were right. You feel all right?"

"It is written," Wu Fang smiled calmly, "that he who boasts of feeling too well should be most careful lest he be near to death. But I have nothing to fear; I have been near to death and always, with the preparations I have made before, I have been able to return to life. So, in defiance of the writings of the most learned ones, I say that I have never felt better in my very eventful life."

WITH THAT, Wu Fang swung his legs off the table and stood up. He was a perfect personification of his tide, Dragon Lord of Crime. He was tall and gaunt with sloping shoulders. His mouth was pinched and narrow, but the upper part of his face above the hideously gleaming green eyes widened to a forehead of great brain capacity.

Wu Fang had no more than risen to his feet when Nee-Sa, the sweet-looking Chinese girl who stood nearest the operating table, rushed forward, bent down, and kissed the feet of the Dragon Lord of Crime. Wu Fang smiled with pleasure.

"Rise, my little yellow bud," he said.

One by one, the other agents came forward, knelt down, and kissed the feet of the yellow devil who held them in his power. Each passed on after his salutation of deep respect, but Nee-Sa remained at Wu Fang's side.

"There is news waiting for me on my return to life?" he asked.

"Yes," the girl nodded. "Gungi is back."

"Gungi?" Wu Fang repeated, frowning for a moment. "Yes, of course. I remember now. He is the messenger who brings word from my agents who are following Mr. Val Kildare and his friend, Mr. Carson. He has good news for me?"

"You shall decide that for yourself, Master," Nee-Sa said.

The girl agents were coming up now to pay their respects to their master. The tall, blond beauty, Tanya, was last. Wu Ring's eyes glowed as he looked at the stately, graceful body of the

Nordic girl. He took hold of her arm as she rose and drew her closer to him.

She seemed like a pawn in his hands, willing to do his bidding. As she looked at him, tears threatened to drop from her lovely blue eyes at any moment, but they were tears of joy and welcome.

"Oh, Master," she said, "we are all so glad that you are back with us."

Wu Fang smiled fondly at the beautiful girl and patted her shoulder gently.

"It makes my heart glad to hear you say that," he said. "You are now my little flower, Tanya, for Mohra has left me. The bonds which held her to me are broken forever. You"—suddenly the yellow fiend clutched Tanya's arm with a force that made her wince—"you will always be true to me, Tanya?"

Tanya nodded in obedience as she replied, "Yes, Master, I will always be true to you."

"I intend to see that you are," Wu Fang said tersely. His flaming eyes flashed about the room, scrutinizing every face for the merest fraction of a second. Then he turned to Nee-Sa. "My whip, Nee-Sa," he said. "Is it not about somewhere?"

The childish face of the Chinese girl lit up with anticipation, for she knew what was coming.

"Yes, Master," she said eagerly. "Your whip is here. I will bring it."

Tanya's lovely blue eyes were wide and staring. There was fear in them now.

"You—you are going to whip someone?" she faltered.

Wu Fang smiled down at her in that fiendishly benign manner peculiar to him. He nodded slowly.

The little beast leaped like a shaft
of lightning toward Gungi.

"Yes, Tanya, I am going to whip someone," he said. "Someone who needs a lesson. Mohra left me. I am going to give you a taste of punishment so that you will not wish to desert me."

9

The girl's face went white with fright.

"But I have always been true to you, Master," she pleaded. "I have always done what you wished."

"Always," Wu Fang smiled, "but once. That was the time you communicated with Mohra without my knowledge. I need not say more. You will remember this."

Nee-Sa returned with a heavy, ugly-looking whip with long rawhide lashes at its end. Still smiling like a delighted child, she handed it to the yellow fiend.

Tanya was clutching at Wu Fang's arm, pleading, going down on her knees.

"Please, please," she begged. "I will always be true to you, Master. I swear it."

Wu Fang had turned his back on her now and was nodding to two of his brown-skinned, half-naked beasts who formed part of the ring about the room. They had officiated at ceremonies like this before and they knew what was expected of them. They leaped forward, each grasping one of Tanya's white arms.

Wu Fang nodded to Nee-Sa and ordered, "Bare her back, my little yellow bud." Even now, his voice had a kindly note in it.

Nee-Sa proceeded to carry out his orders while Tanya's trembling body was held rigid by the two man-beasts. Wu Fang took two steps and turned so that he faced the girl's bare back. Slowly, deliberately, he raised the whip.

There was a crack like that of a pistol shot as the lash descended, and at the very moment that the cruel blow struck, Wu Fang said, "You will remember that, my little flower, when you are tempted to disregard my orders. And you will remember this, too, Tanya."

Crack!

The whip descended again in another stunning blow. Tanya had managed to stifle the cry of pain that had risen to her lips at the first blow, but as that second lash came down on top of the red welts that had risen on her back, she let out a piercing scream of agony.

Again and again Wu Fang lashed her unmercifully until he had counted twenty. Then he calmly handed the whip to Nee-Sa.

"Replace her clothing," be ordered.

Tanya was staggering; she had barely managed to keep from fainting during that awful ordeal.

"Release her," the yellow fiend ordered her two captors. Then he turned to Tanya and grasped her by the shoulders. He smiled down at her white, tear-stained face.

"I am sorry, Tanya," he said apologetically, "but I must enforce my discipline. It is written that lesser pain suffered before temptation will prevent the necessity of greater torture later. And so, while I may appear cruel, my little white flower, I am trying to save you from greater distress later on, in case you should try to disobey me. You understand that, of course."

Tanya bowed her head meekly as she choked, "Yes, Master."

"Very well," the yellow fiend said. "You may go to your room, now." He turned to the doctor and said, "Doctor Wong, you will see that her bruises are attended to immediately so that they will leave no scars."

The Chinese doctor nodded with no sign of expression on his yellow face.

As they left, Wu Fang turned to the others in the room.

"You will all leave me now," he ordered. "All except you, Nee-Sa. You may tell Gungi that I will see him now."

"Yes, Master," the Chinese girl nodded.

SHE TURNED and left the room. A moment later, the drapes through which she had vanished were separated again and she reentered, followed by a wiry little brown man. He was dressed in Occidental clothing and looked as though he possessed a very brilliant mind, but at the same time he moved with the quick, furtive step characteristic of a second-story man.

Wu Fang smiled a greeting.

"You have brought news, Gungi?" he asked.

The little Hindu nodded and smiled back.

"Yes, Master," he said. "I have very important news for you. That is, I think you will consider it important when I have disclosed what it is."

"Wu Fang is waiting," the yellow fiend reminded him "You bring news from Mr. Kildare, do you not?"

Gungi bowed.

"Yes, Master," he said, "but more directly from Mr. Carson, who is working in close contact with Mr. Kildare. It is about the deciphering of certain tablets that Mr. Carson has found in his explorations. He has just learned the key to the ancient language. When he deciphered the messages on the tablets, he discovered a fact that has never been known to the world before."

Wu Fang stood motionless, waiting.

"You know of course about the ancient city of Babylon?" Gungi hurried on.

Wu Fang nodded.

"And you know also of the hanging gardens there?"

Again the yellow fiend nodded.

"But did you know," Gungi asked, "that in building the hanging gardens of Babylon and developing them, Nebuchadnezzar was the first man to develop electricity?"

Wu Fang suddenly grew rigid.

"What did you say?" he demanded. "Electricity in the time of Babylon?"

"Yes, Master," Gungi assured him. "Already Mr. Carson and Mr. Kildare are on their way to Bagdad from London. They were going to travel by steamer and train. I flew to Singapore so that I could bring you the news as quickly as possible."

Wu Fang's face suddenly darkened as he demanded, "You flew to Singapore? That must have made you conspicuous. Was there anyone following you?"

"No, Master, I am sure of it," the little Hindu said.

"Why didn't you send me this news in our secret code, instead of coming yourself?"

"But, Master," Gungi protested, "I thought I should bring you the evidence and all the details as quickly as possible."

"And why, may I ask, do you think that this is so important? Why should you bring me the information that Nebuchadnezzar developed a type of electricity in Babylon?"

"Because, Master," the Hindu said impressively, "I foresee certain things. I foresee death connected with this electricity."

13

"Do you foresee death for anyone else?" Wu Fang asked sharply.

The little Hindu looked perplexed, shook his head.

"No, Master," he said "Why do you ask?"

"It matters little now," Wu Fang retorted. "And the evidence you mentioned—has that anything to do with death or simply the archaeological explorations and the electricity? What has that to do with me?"

"This is a special kind of electricity," Gungi explained. "It is not like any known. I foresee that it will do strange things."

Wu Fang studied Gungi for a moment. Then he smiled.

"You Hindus are quite the brainy people," he purred. "Probably there is no other race on the earth which has such perfect brain and body control!" The yellow fiend shrugged his narrow shoulders as he continued, "You believe you can tell by your visions into the future what will happen, but I, Wu Fang, do not believe in those things. To me, any man who professes to be able to foresee what is going to happen in the future is a fake, for if he were truly capable of that feat, he could make himself the richest and most powerful man in the world."

"But, Master, I have the evidence here," Gungi said. "I have the notes, the interpretation itself, in Mr. Carson's own handwriting. I stole them from his desk."

Wu Fang leaned forward suddenly as the little Hindu produced a few folded papers with writing on them and handed them to his master proudly. The eyes of the yellow fiend blazed savagely as he glanced first at the papers and then at Gungi.

"So you stole these papers from Mr. Carson's desk," he observed.

"Yes, Master," Gungi bowed. His face was taking on a worried look now for his master did not appear nearly as pleased as he had expected.

"And I suppose you committed this burglary very cleverly. After my other agents had followed Mr. Carson and Mr. Kildare so skillfully that they were not aware of it, you stepped in and stole these interpretations of the Babylonian tablets."

"Yes, of course, that was my work," Gungi agreed quickly, hoping that his words would bring a smile to the lips of the yellow fiend. Instead, Wu Fang gravely asked another question.

"Of course, it never occurred to you that it would have been a much better plan to copy the information from these papers and leave them on the desk, so that Mr. Carson would not suspect that anyone besides himself was aware of their contents?"

"But, Master, I—"

Wu Fang held up his hand in a gesture for silence as he continued, "You say the reason for this theft of the papers, and for your opinion that they are of the utmost importance, is that you foresee death in connection with this new type of electricity. In other words, I am to understand that you possess powers of looking into the future?"

The little Hind bowed.

"Yes, Master," he answered, "I see death in connection with this new type of strange electricity that is mentioned on the tablets."

"Then if you can look into the future, Gungi," Wu Fang said

suavely, "look into that future that is closer at hand and tell me what is to happen to you."

GUNGI STARED at the Dragon Lord of Crime for a moment, wide-eyed and frightened.

"I do not know," he faltered, "but I have a strange feeling."

"Yes," Wu Fang nodded, "you have a strange feeling because you can see the truth in my eyes. Can you tell me what I am thinking of—what I am planning?"

Gungi hesitated a moment—a fatal moment for him. He opened his mouth to reply but Wu Fang cut him off.

"No, you can not tell," he said. "You claim to see into the future, but no man alive has the power to do that, except Wu Fang, who makes his own future. You are a faker; you can not even read my mind now."

Then, as Gungi stammered for words, Wu Fang turned to Nee-Sa who stood smiling at his side.

"Tell Djiga I have work for him at once," he said. "I do not wish to waste any time."

Nee-Sa ran off and disappeared behind the folds of a drape. Gungi stared after her, frightened and shaking.

"But, Master," he begged, "what are you going to do to me? What have I done? Djiga is the keeper of the poison beasts, is he not? You are bringing him here to—"

Wu Fang smiled.

"Your powers of perception are improving, Gungi," he said. "You were instructed, when you started on this mission, that under no circumstances was Mr. Carson or Mr. Kildare to suspect that I am still alive. You have bungled your job. You stole the papers instead of copying them as you should have done, and you flew here to Singapore, making yourself conspicuous. I have no tolerance for your ignorance."

Gungi was trembling so that he could hardly stand. He was clutching at Wu Fang's sleeve, pleading, begging. The yellow fiend stepped away, and with a lightning-fast movement, hurled Gungi from him.

With a cry of desperation and rage, the little Hindu leaped to his feet. He was a wiry, fast little fellow and he moved with the speed and ease of a panther. He crouched, ready to spring at Wu Fang. Now was his only chance. His back was to the wall and he was alone with the yellow devil.

He screamed out a threat, "You have done this to others who did their best to serve you faithfully but you will not do it to me. I will kill you first. I will—"

That moment of hesitation cost Gungi dearly, for at that instant the drape through which Nee-Sa had vanished moved, and a figure appeared a short distance behind the little Hindu. This was Djiga, the ugliest and most repulsive of all Wu Fang's brown-skinned agents. As he came into the room, the air was filled with a repulsive stench of filth. He was flat-headed, flat-nosed, short, squat, and powerful. His beady little eyes focused on Gungi and the Hindu whirled around just in time to meet his hideous glare.

In Djiga's right hand nestled a small beast, no larger than a mouse but a thousand times more hideous. As though the little animal could read Djiga's mind, its eyes focused on Gungi and two long, needle-like fangs were bared at the front of the rat-

Carson's right came up in
a slashing uppercut.

like head. But the rest of the body was different; it resembled the body of a scaly frog with its short forelegs and long, powerful, jumping hind quarters.

The little beast leaped as though at a mental command from Djiga—leaped like a shaft of lightning toward Gungi. It stretched out flat and flew straight and swift as an arrow. In spite of Gungi's quick dodge to avert this sudden death, the little beast struck the back of his neck, apparently landing very lightly. In one swift movement, the fangs were embedded in the Hindu's flesh.

As though the fangs had touched off a spring, Gungi's body stiffened, shot up into the air, and landed again as rigid as a marble statue.

Djiga uttered a strange-sounding word and the little frog-beast drew its fangs from Gungi's neck and leaped back on Djiga's shoulder, rubbing its head fondly against its master's neck.

Wu Fang nodded at the corpse on the floor.

"Take him out, Djiga," he ordered.

Djiga grunted and reached down and grasped the Hindu's hair. Then he turned and dragged him from the room.

Without a word, Wu Fang unfolded the papers that Gungi had brought him and read them over. Nee-Sa stood silently by his side, waiting for orders. Several minutes later, when he had finished reading the papers, he looked up at her.

"Perhaps this is important, Nee-Sa," he said. "Perhaps the perceptions of the departed Gungi were correct when he foresaw death mingled with this strange electricity."

Nee-Sa picked up one of Wu Fang's long yellow hands and caressed it as she pleaded, "Master, I have waited for this moment. Kildare and Carson must die so that you will have full sway, with no one to hinder you. Let me be the messenger of death. I will do it cleverly. We will plan it together and when I am through, Mr. Kildare and Mr. Carson will never again stand in your way."

Wu Fang smiled down at the Chinese girl but shook his head firmly.

"Later, of course, Nee-Sa," he said. "But not now. I have use for Mr. Kildare and Mr. Carson. And now that I have read over the deciphered messages on the Babylonian tablets, I have important news for them. Send in my agents, the cleverest ones in my employ. I must also get in touch with my agent in Bagdad. Mr. Kildare and Mr. Carson will be watched constantly from now on. I will have them under control at all times and I will use them as I see fit. When I have finished with them—that will not be more than three days from now at the most—then you shall have your chance, Nee-Sa. You shall finish them."

CHAPTER 2
THE STRANGE
DISAPPEARANCE

"CONFOUND IT, I wish they would do what they're going to do and get it over with. If there's anything that drives me nuts, it's having to wait for someone else to start things. For two cents, I'd go back and pick a fight with those birds just to get it over with."

Those words came from the thin, firm lips of Rod Carson, eminent young explorer and archaeologist. Carson was a well-built, muscular young man of medium height. He had a clean-cut sturdy face above his rock-like jaw. The light that flashed from his deep blue eyes betrayed the restless nature that had led him into all parts of the world in search of ancient treasures.

Even as he spoke, Carson began to turn around in the seat of the railroad coach, but a firm hand on his arm arrested his movement. He looked up into the long, lean face of Val Kildare, former number one investigator of the United States Secret Service. Kildare was smiling, and in that expression, his steady, penetrating gray eyes were narrowed. He sat slumped a little in his seat, his long legs wound one around the other.

"That wouldn't do any good," Kildare said quietly. "After all, Rod, just because those two men have been with us all the way from London is no proof that they're following us."

"All right, but how about that Chinaman, back five seats on the other side of the coach?" Rod Carson challenged defiantly.

Kildare laid his head back against the cushion and smiled.

"I'll grant you that he and the two white men have stuck pretty close to us since we left London nearly two weeks ago."

"But why didn't those two men and the Chink take seats in other coaches?" Carson asked.

"That is quite easy to understand," Kildare continued. "I happened to learn from the conductor that all five of us are headed for Bagdad, according to our tickets."

"And still you don't think that we're being followed by any of them?" Carson demanded.

"I didn't say that," Kildare countered, shaking his head, "but my theory is that the odds are very slight. Nevertheless, we'll be on our lookout."

It was nearing midnight of the second day out from Beirut, Syria, and the train on which Kildare and Carson were passengers was winding in and out across the barren stretch of land that formed the border between northern Syria and Turkey.

After a lapse of several minutes, Rod Carson jerked his head around suddenly and looked at Kildare.

Kildare asked, "What's on your mind?"

Carson hesitated, his face troubled.

"Same old thing, I guess," he said.

"You mean Wu Fang?" Kildare asked.

Carson nodded.

"You're pretty sure he's dead, aren't you?" he asked.

Kildare's eyes narrowed ever so slightly as he answered, "I am never sure of anything in connection with Wu Fang."

"Then you do think he's alive?" Carson probed.

"No," Kildare protested, shaking his head, "I didn't say that."

"You mean to say," Carson challenged, "that the theft of those papers containing the interpretations of the Babylonian tablet inscriptions wasn't definite proof that Wu Fang is still alive?"

"There," Kildare said slowly, "is a question—a chance for argument. Let's go back over that a minute and see if we can figure just what did happen.

"You were in the room next to mine in our London hotel. That evening you had discovered the key to the writings on the tablets which you had found on a previous expedition to the ruins of Babylon. You worked until three o'clock in the morning deciphering them.

"You called me, then, and told me what you had found. Naturally, we were both very much elated about the whole thing. Then I returned to my room and we both turned in for the night.

"When I met you again in the morning, you told me that the papers on which you had deciphered the writings were gone. Someone had slipped into your room during the night and stolen them. We both figured that since those papers had been stolen, Wu Fang must still be alive.

"On the other hand, you said that you had mentioned some of the things that you expected to find on this trip to a London newspaper correspondent, but you refused to give him any definite information because you were saving it for Jerry Hazard. Therefore, you suspected that possibly a reporter might have broken into your room and stolen the papers."

"Sure," Carson said. "We both wanted Jerry Hazard to have the scoop because, since he was crippled and is working with

Mohra's help, it's hard for the poor fellow to get hold of a scoop unless we help. I cabled him the bare facts as I remembered them. His news syndicate must have spread the story all over the world in a hurry because it appeared in the last edition of one of the London papers the next day."

"Right," Kildare said, "and then that evening you went to work and deciphered the tablets again. But—and this is the most puzzling thing of all—those second papers were also stolen."

The government man shook his head slowly in the negative.

"I've known Wu Fang a long time," he said, "and that's one thing that leads me to believe that he isn't in on this thing. Wu Fang doesn't steal the same thing twice. Once his agents take what they've come for, they've got it and they go straight to headquarters."

"Sure," Carson admitted, "but look here. Suppose this agent of Wu Fang lost the first papers. Suppose he was caught stealing them—or was even suspected of it? The natural thing for him to do would be to destroy the papers. In that case, he would have to come back and get another copy."

Kildare shrugged and shook his head.

"No, Rod," he said, "that doesn't make the right kind of sense. Not when you're talking about Wu Fang."

"You still think he's dead then?"

"Here's the only way to look at that angle," Kildare said. "As we go into this new mystery, let us assume that Wu Fang is still alive and that we have to cope with him. That's the safest bet.

Then, if we find that we have no interference from him, we're that much better off.

"By the way, Rod," Kildare continued. "Did you find anything more when you made that third translation of the tablets? I mean, any more definite information on the mystery of that ancient electrical device?"

Carson shook his head.

"NO," HE said, "there was quite enough information given in the other two translations so that I know pretty clearly that we were on the track of something. You have read them, of course?"

"Yes," Kildare said. "Several times, in fact. This is one of the most vitally interesting things I have ever run across. It must be a real thrill to be the first one to uncover things that have been buried for thousands of years—to be the first to learn things that no other modern human being knows."

"It is," Carson assured him. "But we've got to be careful in this. There's a warning note in the translation. I think I got it right, but I had to guess at part of it since there was no duplication of one of the symbols in the key. It's regarding the danger of this electrical device by which Nebuchadnezzar illuminated the hanging gardens that he built for his queen, Semiramis. As near as I could figure it out, the tablets tell of a number of mysterious deaths that occurred in the underground chamber where the machinery for making the light was kept. According to them, all the attendants were killed at one time when the wrath of the gods was bent upon Babylon."

"Have you figured out what was meant by the wrath of the gods?" Kildare asked.

Carson looked thoughtful.

"I've been trying to," he admitted. "Of course, in those ancient days, storms and all kinds of earthly disturbances were said to have been caused by the wrath of the gods."

"Floods might have done it," Kildare reminded him.

"Yes," Carson admitted.

"What are your plans after we reach Bagdad?" Kildare asked.

"I have wired to my headman, Asfar Moez, to make an investigation at once through our old tunnel into the interior of the remains of the hanging gardens. He is to have everything ready to push on from there so that we can search for this underground room where the light was developed. He may have started work by the time we reach there tomorrow evening."

"Do you have any trouble getting the permission of the government for your explorations there?"

"I never have, so far," Carson said. "It takes a little bribery, sometimes. Most of those ruling chiefs or governors like the Amirs and the Pashas are politicians at heart, and they don't mind doing a favor when the bargain is gilded with gold. We won't have to worry about that part of it."

Kildare looked sharply at Carson for a moment. Then he yawned and stretched his long arms.

"I think I will prepare to lie back and get some sleep," he said.

The government man rose and walked down the aisle toward the men's room at the rear of the coach. That gave Carson a chance to turn and stare back into the faces of the two white men behind him, and into that of the Chinaman five seats behind and across the aisle.

The Chinaman was of medium build and his face was narrow and showed evidence of good breeding. He was reading a book at the moment Carson looked at him, but as though he felt the scrutiny, his keen eyes rose and met Carson's for an instant. Immediately, the young explorer shifted his gaze toward Kildare's back. He saw the government man open the door of the men's room, enter, and close it again behind him.

Carson took that occasion to glance at the two men three seats behind him. They were obviously Britishers, he decided. Their faces were hard, but he knew they couldn't be thugs for they had heavily-tanned, leathery skins instead of the usual sallow, pasty complexions of men of that sort.

One of the Britishers was lolling back against his seat and the other had been absently glancing out of the window. The moment Carson glanced at him, he turned quickly and eyed the young explorer with a steady, penetrating gaze.

Carson wished desperately that he could read the man's thoughts. It was very strange that the same five people should make a journey from London to Bagdad on the same boat and train.

But the Chinaman didn't fit into the picture at all. He looked like a suave, scholarly type of Oriental gentleman, and unlike the two Britishers, he had a pleasant, likeable face.

Feeling that he was making himself conspicuous by having

turned around too long, Carson twisted back into his original position and stared out the window once more.

Minutes passed. He glanced at his watch. Yes, fifteen minutes were gone. Why didn't Kildare return? What had happened? He turned around to stare back down the aisle and a suspicion instantly flashed through his mind.

The gentlemanly Chinese was coming down the aisle from the door of the men's room. He looked at Carson, returning the young explorer's scrutiny calmly as he sat down in his seat again and prepared to resume his reading.

Carson turned back and glanced out of the window again. He looked at his watch a few minutes later. Twenty-five minutes had passed since Val Kildare had left him.

Rod Carson's taut nerves demanded action. He leaped from his seat and strode down toward the door at the rear of the coach. He glanced at the Chinaman in passing, but the yellow man merely looked at him calmly and followed the young explorer's back with his olive eyes.

Carson tried the latch on the door to the men's room. It turned easily and he pushed the door in and entered. He stared about blankly, his mouth open in astonishment. Val Kildare was nowhere to be seen.

CHAPTER 3
YELLOW HANDS

F OR ONE instant, Carson stood petrified staring about the interior of the little room. The mirror over the wash

28

basin was cracked and the towel rack was bent in to the wall. His glance shifted to the window and he saw that it was open wide. He leaped across the little space separating him from it and stared out.

There was only the blackness of the night filled with the snort of the engines up ahead and the roar and clank of iron discs thumping over the rails.

He was nearly beside himself in rage and desperation. The whole thing was plain to him now. That wiry Chinaman had followed Kildare into the men's room. A fight had ensued and in some way, doubtless by a drug, the yellow man had overpowered Kildare. Then that smooth Oriental devil who, Carson was positive, now, was an agent of Wu Fang, had finished the government man by pushing him through the open window.

Something at the edge of the window caught Carson's eye. There were a few threads caught on a screw head on the sill. He stared down at them, snatched them loose and inspected them closely. Yes, they were threads from Kildare's tweed suit. They must have caught on the screw head when Kildare was dragged over the sill and hurled to his doom.

The young explorer spun around and headed down the narrow corridor that led to the platform between that car and the one in the rear, yelling for the conductor as he went.

He found himself suddenly face to face with the Chinaman. The Oriental opened his mouth to speak. There was a look of concern and perplexity on his face. All that Carson took to be assumed put on for his benefit. He was half-mad with anger by now. This Chinaman had done away with Kildare. Perhaps he was only waiting his chance to give him the same treatment. Well, he would beat him to it.

Carson lashed out with his right hand and then his left as he snarled, "You lousy, yellow skunk! You think you're going to catch me off guard as you did Kildare."

Wham!

His left fist connected.

Crack!

The right caught the Chinaman on the chin and hurled him back. He caught hold of the seats and partially saved himself from falling. He was trying to speak.

"What is the cause of this sudden—"

That was as far as he got for Carson was upon him, his left hand gripping the front of the neat coat that the yellow man wore.

"So you threw Kildare out of the window, did you?" he rasped.

Carson hesitated an instant before he struck, for the Chinaman seemed truly baffled and frightened. But again, Carson realized that it was probably all acting on the Oriental's part.

"Excuse me," the Chinaman said politely, placing his hand on Carson's wrist and trying to move him away. "If you will release me," he said, "I will try to tell you what little I know."

Carson let go of the man's clothing but he kept his right fist clenched.

"All right," he snapped. "Make it fast. What do you know about it?"

"I was planning to go to the men's room," the Oriental said, "but at that moment the chap who was sitting with you left his

30

seat and walked down the aisle. I decided to wait until he returned and began reading again. After several minutes had passed, I thought perhaps he had come out and gone into the coach behind without my seeing him, so I got up and went down to the lavatory myself. I was just coming back when you saw me sitting down again in my seat."

Carson's eyes narrowed suspiciously as he demanded, "You mean you didn't see Kildare when you went into the men's room? You didn't notice anything strange?"

The Chinaman shook his head.

"I am very sorry," he said, "but I can not help you further. You see, I never entered the men's room at all. When I tried the door, it was locked."

"Locked!" Carson cried. "You're a liar! It was open just now when I entered. You're trying to get by with a crazy alibi. Well, you're not going to do it."

Once more the young explorer's temper got the best of him and his right fist shot forward, catching the yellow man squarely between the eyes. The Chinaman's knees sagged from the terrific force of the blow.

Carson tried to jerk him up, but the yellow man was out cold. By this time, other passengers in the car were coming down to interfere. The two white men, who had been with Carson and Kildare ever since they had left London, were in the lead.

"Hey, what's going on?" the larger one demanded.

"Yes," the other one—a short, stocky man—growled. "What's the idea of picking on this Chink?"

Carson's eyes blazed and he stepped over the fallen Oriental to face them.

"I've had my eye on you two as well as the Chinaman," he rasped. "Maybe you'd like it better if I picked on you."

There was room in the aisle for only one man to stand at a time, so the two Britishers couldn't stand abreast. Without the slightest hesitation, Carson whipped out his left fist toward the big fellow who was in the lead and crashed a thudding blow to his stomach. There was a grunt and the larger of the two Britishers doubled over. At that moment, Carson's right came up in a flashing uppercut and the big fellow's head snapped back and he staggered.

The short, stocky man muscled his way past his comrade and came charging at Carson, who was having the time of his life. He let go another left that caught the short man on the temple even as he ducked. He let his head roll with the blow, but Carson's right followed so swiftly that it caught him between the eyes in the same manner that it had hit the Chinaman. The stocky man wobbled, his knees bent, and he went reeling over into a vacant seat at the side.

Carson ducked as something flashed toward his face. He hadn't noticed that the big fellow had straightened again; his eyes had been concentrated solely on the short man for the moment.

Wham!

SOMETHING STRUCK Carson on the side of his head with the power of a sledge. It was the right fist of the big fellow. The dim lights of the coach danced and went out for an instant.

As his head began to clear, Carson struggled to his feet. He heard the big fellow say something and the next instant one of his arms was pinned behind his back. The short, stocky man seized the other and held on to it.

"I heard you call the Chinaman a liar when he told you the door was locked," the big fellow was saying. "My friend and I can tell you that he was not lying."

Carson's rage was suddenly leaving him, and his usual calm judgment was returning. He shook his head, rubbed his jaw.

"Wait a minute," he said. "Things are pretty hazy yet."

"Things are hazy for all of us," the big fellow retorted. "You've got plenty of fight in you, fellow, but there's no need of getting sore at us. We haven't anything to do with the trouble you're in. Now what's all this argument about?"

Carson stared at the big man and then at his shorter companion. The Chinese was quite calm in spite of the split flesh on his chin and over one eye. Oddly enough, he seemed to bear no resentment toward Carson.

"If I may explain," he said, "I believe the gentleman is under a delusion. From what I gather, his friend has disappeared from the men's room and he is blaming me for it."

The big fellow looked at his companion with a strange, perplexed expression on his face, glanced questioningly at Carson.

"You mean to say that the chap who was sitting with you— the tall, lanky one—isn't on the train?"

Carson jerked his head toward the open door of the men's room.

"Come in and take a look for yourselves," he said hoarsely. "I saw my friend come in here about a half hour ago. You all saw him get up and come down the aisle from his seat, didn't you?"

The two white men and the Chinaman nodded.

"I saw him go in and close the door," Carson continued. "Look at the place now."

He led them into the room and pointed at the broken mirror over the wash basin, the bent towel rack and the open window. He still held the few wisps of thread that he had wrenched loose from the screw head.

"I found these," he said, holding them up, "on that screw head outside the window."

Again he saw the two Britishers exchange puzzled glances.

"I say," the short one observed, "it looks as though there had been a fight in here."

At that moment the train conductor, a swarthy Turk, entered the coach. Carson remembered that he spoke a little English, so he told him what had happened.

"If you ask me, conductor," he finished, "these three men"—he pointed to the two tanned Englishmen and the Chinaman—"are working together."

"Wait," the short man protested quickly. "Simply because we all happen to be bound for the same destination is no reason why this fellow should suspect that we're plotting against him."

"Of course," the big fellow chimed in. "He's making a mistake."

"One minute, please," the Turkish conductor said.

"Look here," Carson said, "I demand that these two Englishmen and the Chinaman be placed under arrest and that the train be stopped and backed up so that we can search for my friend who has been thrown off."

"Please, please," the conductor begged. "I take charge. I ask the questions. You say your friend thrown out of window? How do you know?"

"I just know," Carson cried. "I found these threads"—he held them up and shook them in the Turk's face—"on the edge of the window. That Chinaman came back here while my friend was in the men's room. I saw him when he returned to his seat. He swears that he never entered the room and that the door was locked when he tried it. I came back here a few minutes later and it was unlocked."

"The Chinaman told the truth," the big Englishman interrupted. "We saw the Chinaman going down the aisle. I watched him myself as he tried the door. When he found it was locked, he returned to his seat. That's the truth and I'll swear to it."

"For the love of heaven!" Carson cried. "Don't you understand? He's probably lying beside the track somewhere, unconscious!" Carson went on. "He may be dying. I demand that you stop this train at once and that we back up and search for him!"

The Turk conductor shrugged and shook his head.

"No," he said emphatically. "It would be quite useless, I assure you."

"Useless?" Carson snarled. "What are you talking about?"

"One minute, please," the conductor said. "I explain."

He turned and motioned toward the side of the car away from the open window.

"For the last hour we pass along edge of Keffa Mountains," he said. "If your friend go out on that side, he roll under wheels of train." He shrugged and pointed toward the open window. "There mountain drop straight down from the track for almost three thousand feet. If your friend fall out of window, he is dead. No need to turn back."

CHAPTER 4
THE TRAIL OF DEATH

THE TRAIN pulled into Mosul in the morning. Carson had caught a few winks of sleep, but his spinning brain would permit no more than that. He had argued half the night with the conductor, trying to make him stop the train. He had even tried to bribe him, but the Turk would not yield.

Carson angrily choked down the lump that rose in his throat. That Chinaman was responsible for Kildare's disappearance! He was positive of that and he was willing to bet that those two white men were accomplices.

As the train pulled into Mosul, Carson found the Turkish conductor and said, "I demand the arrest of these three men and the holding of the rest of the passengers on this car as witnesses."

"You not need to worry," the conductor said. "I see to that myself. All of you are under arrest until this matter is solved. I take charge myself."

"Are we to leave the train at Mosul?" Carson asked.

The conductor shook his head.

"No," he said, "all tickets read for Bagdad, so we go there. I keep this coach locked while train stops at Mosul. Food will be brought in to you. Police await train arrival in Bagdad."

"Fine," Carson said.

Sandwiches and preserved fruits were passed as the train stopped in Mosul. Carson managed to down a few sandwiches, although he hadn't much appetite after what had happened.

All day long, the train tore on down out of the mountains and through the great fertile plateau between the Tigris and Euphrates rivers. Then as evening fell, they pulled into that famous city of Bagdad.

A dozen swarthy, dark-skinned police officers surrounded the coach the moment the train pulled in. Carson and the others were taken at once to a court, a surprising thing to any American who was accustomed to seeing court actions delayed for weeks while the suspects were held in jail.

There was a rapid questioning with the Turk conductor acting as interpreter. The two Englishmen and the Chinaman stuck to their stories. The passengers had seen nothing, according to their statements. Carson repeated his suspicions, but it all seemed to make little impression on the brown-skinned judge who sat glowering at them.

The entire testimony was finished in less than an hour. At the end of that time, the judge rose and shrugged his shoulders. He said something in his native tongue but he talked so rapidly that Carson couldn't understand what he said.

"He says no cause for action," the Turk conductor explained. "Your friend must have fallen out of window. You all go home."

"All go home!" Carson exclaimed. "What are you talking about? Why, the judge is crazy."

He whirled around toward the man officiating as judge and cried, "Say, you—"

He broke off suddenly, for he saw the judge was gone. He had vanished through the door behind his chair after finishing his short speech.

Completely baffled, Carson went to the station and arranged for his baggage to be brought to the hotel where he usually stayed.

"Yes, Mr. Carson, we have made reservations already for you," the clerk at the desk said. "Here is a letter for you that was left a few days ago."

Carson took the letter, glanced at it, recognized the handwriting. The letter was from Asfar Moez. When the servant had left his bags in his room, he tore open the letter and read it. It was written in the easily legible hand of Asfar, the head man of his expedition. It said:

I HAVE DONE AS YOU ORDERED. THE OLD TUNNEL HAS BEEN OPENED ONCE MORE. THE DIGGING HAS GONE AHEAD ACCORDING TO YOUR DIRECTIONS. I HAVE FOUND A LOWER ROOM THAT IS REACHED THROUGH THE LID OF A GREAT STONE CHEST. I HAVE SEEN THE MOST AMAZING THING THERE THAT I HAVE EVER WITNESSED. WOULD ADVISE YOU TO COME AT ONCE UPON YOUR ARRIVAL. I WILL BE WORKING THERE

IN THE LOWER PASSAGE.

Carson's heart began pounding faster for a moment as the exhilaration of new conquests took his mind off Kildare's mysterious disappearance. The exhilaration faded as he began to wonder once more what had happened to the government man.

There was only one solution. That Chinaman had thrown him out of the window. Carson was dead sure of that. He turned quickly as a sound came from behind him. It had come from the other side of that door that opened from his rooms into the adjacent suite.

As he watched, Carson saw that the door was opening slowly. He stepped back a pace; he was too close to the door for quick action. He fumbled for his gun and brought it out in a flashing move.

"Sssh! Don't speak, Carson."

The order came in a hoarse whisper, then a full figure was standing before him. Both the figure and the voice were familiar, but the face was dark and swarthy. But the eyes, the features—

INSTANTLY, ROD CARSON recognized the man and he uttered a low gasp of astonishment.

"Good Lord, Kildare," he said. "How did you get here in that outfit?"

Kildare leaped forward, raising his fingers to his lips.

"Not so loud, Rod," he hissed.

Carson's mind was in a mad whirl.

"What in the name of heaven is the idea?" he demanded. "You nearly scared the life out of me, Kildare. How did you get out of the train without being killed? How did you get here? Did that Chinaman—"

Kildare was shaking his head and chuckling.

"No," he interrupted, "that poor Chinaman had nothing to do with it. You didn't know it, but I was down to the station to meet you. Perhaps you thought it was strange that the judge exonerated everyone so quickly."

"You mean you fixed that, too?" Carson demanded.

Kildare nodded.

"A few pieces of gold will do a lot with these native judges," he said. "After all, there wasn't any use causing a lot of trouble."

Carson took a long breath and dropped into a chair. He shook his head helplessly.

"I don't get any of this," he said in a low voice.

Kildare sat down beside him as he said, "I'll explain everything. I didn't want to admit it on the train, Rod, but I agree with you that we are being followed."

"By the Chinaman?" Carson asked quickly.

Kildare smiled again.

"That poor yellow devil has been in for plenty of blame," he said. "What happened after I left?"

Carson told him.

"You shouldn't have done that, Rod," Kildare said, shaking his head. "That temper of yours is going to get you in trouble some day, I'm afraid. Did the Chinaman resist?"

"Resist?" Carson asked. "Why, he didn't have a chance. I hit him before he knew what was coming. I was so wild at the

Carson gasped as he recognized the figure.

thought that he had thrown you off the train that I saw red. What happened to you?"

"As I told you on the train," Kildare said, "it isn't like Wu

Fang or any of his agents to steal two copies of the deciphered tablets. One would have been plenty, and I have an idea that if Wu Fang had had his way about it, not even one copy would have been stolen. He would have had the information copied and the papers left right there where they were so that you would not know they had been touched. But, nevertheless, they were stolen twice. That leads me to believe that if Wu Fang is alive, he is behind this thing, but he's not the only one. There are two opposing factions, both working against us.

"At any rate, as I said in the beginning, I agree with you that the Chinaman, or the two well-tanned Britishers, or perhaps all three of them have followed us all the way from London.

"I didn't want to admit it to you on the train. I realized that you were pretty well worked up over the thing and I was afraid you would cause a lot of commotion, so I decided to vanish."

"I know," Carson said, "but for heaven's sake, Kildare, why couldn't you have told me?"

"No, Rod," Kildare smiled. "It wouldn't have gone over nearly as well. You wouldn't have seemed as definite, for you're not a very good actor.

"Here's what I wanted to do. Assuming that the Englishmen and the Chinaman are both following us, and at the same time opposing each other in doing so, I wanted each to think that possibly the other had something to do with my disappearance. That's why I stayed in the men's room and kept it locked so long.

"I hoped that both parties would come back and try the door, but as it was, only the Chinaman did. I had waited so long that

I was afraid you would come back and crash down the door yourself, so I left."

"How did you know that the Chinaman came back to the door?" Carson demanded.

"Well, someone tried the door," he said. "When he left, I looked through the keyhole, and from that same keyhole, I could look down the aisle. I saw you turn around and watch the Chinaman as he came back to his seat. I could tell from the expression on your face that you were worried and I knew you would be coming down the aisle before long, so I didn't wait. I tore a few threads from my suit and fastened them to the screw head on the window ledge to make my disappearance look more real. I broke the mirror, catching the pieces of glass in a towel so they wouldn't make so much noise. The train was making plenty of racket anyway to drown out other noises. Then I bent the towel rack in toward the wall."

"But how under the sun did you get out of the train without being killed? How did you get here?"

"I didn't leave the train," Kildare explained, smiling broadly. "I climbed out of the window, and with the aid of the ventilator pipe leading out of the men's room, I reached the top of the coach. I went on back to the top of the last car, and just before the train pulled into Mosul this morning, I dropped off, walked into Mosul, hired the only plane there and flew to Bagdad. I got in here a little before noon."

"And since noon, what have you been doing?" Carson asked.

"I have been making some investigations," Kildare said. "Your man, Asfar Moez, so his wife tells me, hasn't been home for two days—not since he wrote you a note and returned to investigate the remains of the hanging gardens.

"I HIRED a car to drive me to the gardens early this afternoon. I found them guarded by Mohammedan soldiers who told me that someone had ordered the passages kept closed. This happened only within the last forty-eight hours, since Asfar went back to them.

"I got the American consul to go and see the British representative, but he said he could get nothing out of him."

Carson's brow was furrowed as he stared at Kildare with a puzzled expression on his face.

"But why," he asked, "would they want to stop my exploration of the hanging gardens? I'm the only one who has explored them for ten years. I turned up some very valuable treasures that I donated to the little museum here in Bagdad, at my own expense. Why should they want to stop me now?"

Kildare shrugged.

"That's one of the things I mean to find out," he admitted.

A knock sounded on Kildare's hall door and the government man returned to his own room to answer it. A moment later, he returned with a tray of food.

"I ordered supper sent up," he said. "Thought probably you'd be hungry. I know I'm nearly starved. As soon as we eat, we'll be on our way."

"But I thought you said that orders had been given to stop all operations?"

"I have something that I'm going to try," Kildare said. "If they were British soldiers guarding it, I wouldn't attempt it, but these native troops are quite susceptible to bribery if you make the right approach."

After a hurried meal, Kildare rose.

"I'll be going," he said. "You walk to the second corner on the right after you leave the hotel entrance. Hire the car that you see there."

"But where will you be?" Carson asked.

Kildare smiled.

"Never mind me," he said. "I'll be coming along. Tell the driver you want to be taken at once to the hanging gardens."

The government man turned and went into his own room. He locked the door from his side. Carson heard him go out into the hall. A moment later, he followed as Kildare had directed. A block from the hotel, he turned and looked back.

It was so dark that Carson couldn't tell whether anyone was following him or not. He thought he saw, vaguely, a shadowy form stepping out near the entrance of the hotel after he had passed. But then, there had been others walking about the streets.

Two blocks away he found the car that Kildare had mentioned. He stopped beside it.

"I want to be taken to the ruins of the hanging gardens of Babylon, at once," Carson ordered.

The driver nodded.

Carson opened the back door and climbed into the rear seat as the car began to move on. They wound slowly through the narrow, crowded streets and out of town. The driver had not spoken a word since they had started, but now he turned around and said, "You would probably be more comfortable up here with me, Rod."

Carson jerked upright with astonishment as he recognized the driver as none other than Kildare in his Moslem disguise. He changed seats and they jolted on down the sandy roads together.

More than an hour elapsed. A mountain appeared in the distance, silhouetted clearly against the starlit sky. It was El Kasr, all that remained of what once had been one of the seven wonders of the world.

As they drew nearer to it, their headlights shone on a small opening at the side of the hill.

"That's funny," Kildare said.

"You mean the fact that there are no guards visible?" Carson ventured.

Kildare nodded.

"Maybe they're sleeping," he said. "Look, there's something on the ground."

Carson pointed over to the left where a dull light glowed.

"That looks as though it might be their camp fire," he said.

Suddenly, Kildare grasped Carson's arm and turned off the switch of the motor.

"See that?" he said. "Someone moved in that opening at the bottom of the mountain."

Carson nodded; he had seen it too. It was a face that appeared chalk-like in the glare of the headlights.

"I'll turn off the lights," Kildare said. "I'd rather work in the dark, using my electric torch if necessary."

The two got out and crept forward in the darkness. Each had an automatic in one hand and a flashlight in the other. Kildare's light went on suddenly and shot down toward the ground.

"Carson," the government man whispered tensely, "these are the guards, but they're not asleep. They're dead!"

CHAPTER 5
CAVES OF DOOM

KILDARE WAS bending down beside the fallen form of a native soldier.

"Carson," he breathed, "turn your light on the passage opening and keep it trained there. I want to look this fellow over."

Carson was watching the entrance as the beam of his light struck into the black hole. A shadowy thing like a bat flying low seemed to flash in the lower part of his light beam for a moment.

Kildare was speaking again in his low, calm voice.

"No mark of blood at all," he said. "Not a mark of any kind on the face or neck. Nothing on the hands or wrists either. But wait a minute! Here's something! This man is a victim of Wu Fang! There are marks on his leg just above the ankle, two tiny ones. One of Wu Fang's death beasts got him."

"I can see others here too," Carson said, "in the reflection of my light."

The government man rose and flashed his light about. His white-burnoosed figure flitted from one figure to another while Carson kept his flashlight riveted on the opening. In each case he found that the same thing had happened. Fang marks in the leg of each man just above the ankle.

"Come on," he said after he had finished his examination. "If you ever moved with caution, do it now. You'd know Asfar the minute you saw him, wouldn't you?"

"Absolutely," Carson answered.

"All right then, you go first. If anything moves ahead of you, shoot to kill. I'll be right beside you. I'm afraid, though, that we won't find Asfar alive."

They moved toward the opening, which was nearly wide enough for the two to walk abreast. Kildare's light shone on the walls and floor of the passage while Carson kept his turned on the way ahead. Down—down they moved.

Suddenly there was a cry from down ahead of them—a weird, ear-splitting scream of fear and torment. At the first sound of that cry, Kildare leaped ahead and Carson followed him as the government man plunged down the steep incline on a dead run.

"Look out!" the young explorer warned. "The ceiling of the passage is lower here. Don't hit your head."

"I see it," Kildare cried.

There was another scream from just ahead, then their lights probed a dimly illuminated interior. The lower room into which they were racing was familiar to Carson. He and Asfar and his gang of excavators had uncovered it months before.

In the middle of the room, which measured about forty feet square, stood a great stone chest. The cover was made of a slab of rock and it was in this chest that Carson had found trinkets and small statues and bits of jewelry, but he had never gone beyond that point.

Now Carson knew from his translation of the inscriptions on the tablets that another passage led from the false bottom of this stone chest into a chamber below—a chamber that held the mystery and a wonder of the world far greater than the hanging gardens of Babylon themselves.

The lid of the chest was raised now and standing against a stone prop at its back.

To his horror, Carson saw that the chest was swarming with the savage little beasts of Wu Fang—horrible little creatures of every deadly species. There were snakes coiling and striking, and there were also the beasts that combined the frog, the scaly lizard and the rat.

Two men were trying savagely to fight off the animals. They were the two Englishmen who had followed Kildare and Carson all the way from London.

The larger of the two Englishmen was staggering back as a beast leaped to his throat. A snake was striking at his leg and he was reeling, going down.

The short, stocky one was trying to tear away, beating savagely at the attacking beasts with a club.

Phantom shapes leaped out of the shadows at the corner of the room. Something brushed past Carson's ear. Kildare pulled him aside and ducked down.

Carson recognized those shapes as they came out into the light. They were agents of Wu Fang—Chinamen and half-na-

Kildare's gun spoke as Carson struggled.

51

ked brown-skinned devils. They began yelling and jabbering as though they were encouraging the beasts.

The big Englishman had fallen. His body quivered and lay still. The short one darted toward Kildare and Carson, screaming at the top of his voice.

"Stop them!" he yelled. "Don't let them get me!"

"We'll save you if we can," Kildare cracked out.

Then the government man did a strange thing. As the stocky Englishman passed him heading for the entrance, Kildare spun around with his right arm upraised. It came down swiftly and there was a sharp crack as his gun struck the skull of the short man. As his body crumpled, Kildare seized the club and left the man lying where he was.

Blam!

Carson's gun exploded straight at a yellow coolie who had leaped for him out of the shadows.

Wham! Wham!

The club that Kildare had taken from the stocky Englishman beat a resounding tattoo on the floor. A frog-like little monster came flying through the air at the government man.

The young explorer yelled to Kildare, "Lookout!"

AT THE same time, he struck at it with his automatic, caught it in mid-air and hurled it against the side of the room twenty feet away.

Then, suddenly, his arm was wrenched behind him and doubled. For an instant he thought it was going to break under the terrific pressure. Kildare's automatic spoke out, and Carson found that his arm had been released again. The government man had shot his attacker.

More beasts were coming at him. He had his flashlight down, shining it on them as he shot.

"Don't waste your bullets!" Kildare yelled, "Jump on them with your feet. Save your bullets for the devils that—"

Blam!

Again Kildare's gun barked out and was followed by a scream of horror and pain. Carson was fighting like mad. He saw brown and yellow men run toward him. He pulled the trigger again and again but the gun exploded only once. It was empty.

Carson was in the middle of the room beside the chest that still swarmed with the death beasts. His flashlight showed one perched on the upraised cover. It leaped for him. He struck at it and ducked, but he was not fast enough and the thing landed on his left shoulder. Carson swung his right hand and the empty gun came crashing down on his shoulder with savage force. A death scream came from the ugly little animal and it dropped to the floor.

Carson's left hand went limp. A half-naked Malayan gripped him from the left side and tried desperately to get at his gun arm. But that one was still working and Carson brought it down on the skull of his assailant.

Wham!

He felt the gun butt sink into the Malayan's skull. The savage let go and dropped to the floor.

Something struck Carson from behind. He couldn't tell how Kildare was making out, for he didn't have time to turn around.

Wham!

Kildare's gun spoke again as Carson was going down. He tried to catch himself, but the weight of the heavy demon on his back bore him to the floor. But the body was lifeless now; Kildare's bullet had gone home.

Something leaped with all four feet on Carson's face. He knocked it off with his automatic as he struggled to his feet. His light was out; it was somewhere there on the floor where he had dropped it. He could still see, however, for the room was filled with a dim, purplish glow and Kildare still had his flash turned on.

A Chinaman was leaping through the air at him from the side just as he was getting up. Carson ducked to the side, crouched and hurled his automatic through the air with his right hand. His aim was not true and his gun came down on the yellow man's shoulder. He shot out his left arm, to which some of the feeling had returned, and caught the Chinaman on the jaw, but the powerful right arm of the yellow man grabbed Carson by the shoulder and hurled him back.

He heard Kildare utter a warning cry, and at the same time he saw the Chinaman coming for him again. He was diving head first, charging like a wild bull.

Carson couldn't get away and he was off balance. He leaped into the air to avoid that charge and his right arm slashed the air with his gun.

Wham!

The heavy butt caught the Chinaman behind the ear and

sank into the flesh and bone. The head of the agent snapped over and his body sagged to the floor like a rag doll.

Carson flew to help Kildare, for he could see the government man was in trouble. A beast—one of those horny toads with a rat-like head—was flying at him through the air.

A brown-skinned devil had hold of Kildare's left arm and was trying to keep out of range of the government man's gun that he still clutched in his right hand. At the same time, a flat-headed, powerful brute was leaping at Kildare from behind.

The Malayan that had hold of Kildare was yelling in his native tongue, but Carson could catch only one word, "Djiga". That was probably the name of that flat-headed beast.

Carson swung his gun arm, but he was too close to hit it with the gun and caught the flying toad with his wrist.

Splotch!

The beast spattered on the stone floor. Carson jerked Kildare's outstretched gun arm and leaped to the right. At that instant, Kildare managed to duck, but the flat-headed brown man caught him around the knees, sending him to the floor.

Then suddenly, the flat-headed one was screaming something in a jargon of strange tongues, screaming orders that seemed to give the half dozen beasts, still swarming the place, a new fury.

Kildare's automatic hand was flying again. It caught the brown man on the side of the jaw and hurled him back.

Carson grabbed Kildare under the arm, but the government man was already getting up. Holding fast to the young explorer's arm, he pulled him over to the other side of the room that seemed to be free from attacking beasts and brown and yellow human devils.

"Give me some more clips for my gun," he snapped. "Somebody took mine from my pocket."

Carson shot his hand into his pocket, brought out the one clip he had brought with him. He poured it out.

"Here," he said.

But before Kildare could get it, something whirled through the air. The government man caught a charging little beast with his empty automatic as another struck Carson in the chest. Kildare brought his gun up and crushed the little lizard-like beast against Carson's ribs.

Then suddenly, Kildare pitched forward on his face. Carson whirled around to see what had struck him, and came face to face with the flat-headed man who was leaping at him with a club in his hand. Carson dodged, but he couldn't avoid that descending weapon.

Wham!

There was a crash as though his brain had burst, a spatter of star-dust, and then the engulfing blackness of night.

CHAPTER 6
THE COOKED CORPSE

S OMETHING WAS groping over Rod Carson. That was his first realization that he was at all conscious again. Then he was aware of a terrific throbbing in his head as though his skull were a gigantic drum upon which someone was beating.

Carson became aware of a strange, very faint odor in the place. Was it incense or perfume? He couldn't tell.

Now, suddenly, he felt a hand on his neck. It was cold and clammy, like the hand of a corpse and it reached up and rubbed falteringly across his cheek ever so softly. The hand was weak and flabby; weakness was the cause of its gentle movement.

With a frantic effort, Rod Carson moved his head away. The hand dropped past his ear and fell into the place where his head had been. Carson moved his own fingers and for the first time he realized that he was lying flat on his back on a cold stone floor.

He heard a very weak, faint voice say, "Carson, Rod Carson. Are you—conscious? Is that you?"

Carson recognized the weak voice as that of Kildare, and he felt the body of the government man moving closer against his side. Kildare was crawling along the floor like a wounded animal.

The young explorer's lips seemed to be stuck together, but with an effort, he managed to whisper, "Yes, this is Rod. What happened? Are you all right?"

"I think so," came Kildare's voice again, closer to his ear, but still very weak. "I thought I could see you lying there. Hard work—to get over to you."

"See me?" Carson gasped. "But its pitch dark in here."

"No," Kildare whispered. "I thought so, too—at first. I can see—you now in the purple light. It's very dim—weird, but I can make you out. Your eyes—are stuck shut. Mine were too. Here—let me help."

And now Carson felt the cold weak fingers of the government

man on the lids of his left eye. He had his own right hand to the other. Kildare was right. The eyelids were stuck shut. Gradually, painfully, he forced them open.

"There that's better," Kildare was saying.

Carson could see dimly now. He noticed that there was a dim, purple light illuminating the place. It seemed to have no definite source; but it was as though every particle of atmosphere radiated a dull, purple glow.

He rolled his head and looked about. He saw Kildare lying on the stone floor beside him. They must be in an underground room—perhaps the same place where they had been knocked out, that chamber with the death beasts and the chest of stone. But while Carson could see some other things, he couldn't find the stone chest.

There was wreckage strewn about and as he turned his head completely to the right, he made out another form lying perhaps six or seven feet from him. The sight of it gave even Carson a sickly chill. The body didn't look human or normal. Was it wasted away—half-rotted? That was strange, though, because if the body were decayed, it should be giving off an odor. The eyes were horrible with their dull, flabby stare.

Then as Carson recognized the body he cried out, "Asfar!"

"Is that who it is?" Kildare asked, rising just enough so that he could look over Carson's body.

Carson nodded.

"Yes," he said in a low voice, "that's Asfar. He must have been dead a long rime."

"Something queer about it," Kildare said. "Everything is strange down here."

"Do you know where we are?" Carson asked.

"I have an idea," Kildare said, "that we're in the lower chamber of the hanging gardens where the electrical appliance was located. That's where Asfar was going, wasn't it?"

"Yes," Carson admitted, "I am sure that's where we are."

"Feeling any stronger?" Kildare asked.

"Gradually," Carson said.

"Take it easy," Kildare advised. "Every time I move I can hear my heart pounding pretty hard. There's something that's pretty bad on the heart down here. Let's lie back and relax until we feel a little more normal. No use jumping up and having our hearts work themselves to death."

"How long have we been here?" Carson asked as he lay back.

"No telling," Kildare said. "I regained consciousness just a few minutes ago. We may have been here for an hour or for several days."

"It seems as though it must have been weeks by the way I feel," Carson said.

"I didn't think a blow on the head could have made me feel so weak."

"No," Kildare said, "I think it was something else. We were meant to die here. Smell that odor, a sort of combination of perfume and incense?"

"Yes," Carson said, "I smelled it when I first came to."

"I think that's the cause of our weak feeling," Kildare said. "They've thrown us down in this lower chamber and turned some kind of a strange gas on us. Evidently, it didn't quite do the trick. Perhaps it was light and clung to the ceiling and since we were on the floor, we didn't receive its most deadly effects."

CARSON LAY back and remained limp for several minutes, but the old restlessness was coming over him again. He turned his head and looked over at Kildare.

"What are you planning to do?" he asked.

"I'm feeling stronger," Kildare said. "How about you?"

"Right," Carson agreed.

"Well, here's what I have in mind. Doubtless the trap door that leads out of here through the bottom of the stone chest is closed to keep the gas fumes in this room. If we can get that open so that they will pass off, we'll be O.K."

"But they'll hit you with their deadly effects," Carson protested.

"Not if I can keep from breathing until we finish the job," Kildare said.

Carson sat up decisively.

"I'm going with you," he said.

"All right. Let's go."

Kildare sat up and pointed to stone steps that rose to the ceiling of the underground room. "Look over there," he said. "The trap door is at the top of those stairs. Here." He picked up a heavy club. "This ought to do for a wedge to hold the door open," he said. "Come on. Take a deep breath and then hold it. Don't breathe until we get back here."

They crawled rapidly across the floor on all fours, and reached the top of the stairs. Kildare was prying at the door. Carson stuck his fingers in the crevice and pulled down. The stone bottom of the great chest above opened without too much effort.

Neither man spoke, as they were holding their breaths. Carson could feel his heart pounding rapidly at the base of his skull. They would have to hurry; he was getting very dizzy. He held the door down as far as he could, while Kildare put the stick in it. Immediately they became aware of a gentle draft of air passing them.

Carson started back down the stairs, growing dizzier and dizzier. His lungs fell as though they would burst from lack of air. Once more on the floor at the bottom of the steps, he took a long, satisfying breath.

"O.K.?" he heard Kildare hiss a moment later.

"Yes," Carson gasped.

"I think that draft will take care of all the deadly fumes," Kildare said.

Cautiously, Carson sniffed the air. The smell of mingled perfume and incense was not nearly so strong now.

Kildare got up on his hands and knees and Carson followed suit.

"First I want to have a look at Asfar," the government man said, "to see what actually happened to him."

They crawled over to the corpse. Asfar's body was a ghastly sight. The dim, purple glow that filled the place shone its weird light on the native's flesh. He was dressed like any of the other Moslems and lay in a twisted heap, partly on his side and partly on his back. His face was turned to the side.

61

Carson touched his cheek with his fingers, drew back suddenly with a shudder. The flesh on the cheek bone had moved, but at the same time it was cold and clammy.

"Good Heavens, Kildare, he's rotted already," Carson cried. "Either something very unusual has happened to him or we've been unconscious for days. The human body doesn't rot as quickly as this, does it?"

"No," Kildare said, "particularly in a cool, dry place like this."

The government man was feeling of the flesh, tearing away the white clothing from the shoulders and neck. Then suddenly he stopped and Carson saw that he was staring over the body at an object lying on the floor. It was an electric flashlight containing three or four cells.

"Funny," Kildare said. "He was carrying a flashlight when whatever killed him came along."

He reached over and picked up the electric torch, looked at if for a moment, but made no effort to turn it on. Suddenly, he laid it back on the floor where it had been. Carson reached for it, but Kildare's hand restrained him.

"I wouldn't do it," the government man said.

"Wouldn't do what?" Carson demanded.

"I don't know," Kildare said perplexedly. "Perhaps it's just one of my funny hunches, but do you remember that part of the tablet inscriptions that you deciphered about the wrath of the gods descending upon the attendants down here and killing them?"

"Yes," Carson nodded, "but what could that have to do with the flashlight?"

"Have you figured out what the wrath of the gods might mean?" Kildare asked.

"Sure," Carson said. "It might mean a storm, a flood, or even an earthquake."

"Right," Kildare said, "and it might mean a particular kind of a storm. How about a thunder storm?"

Carson stared at him.

"But after all, there's nothing so mysterious about anybody being killed by lightning."

"Lightning," Kildare said, "isn't apt to kill people a hundred feet under the ground. Not normally, anyhow. Lightning is electricity, or at least has to do with it, and so do electric flash-lights. Look, here's something else, too."

Kildare was pulling the clothing down over the shoulders of the gruesome dead body. He probed around with his fingers.

"Wait," he said, "I can't tell anything by this light. I want to look into something else. Then I'll explain what I mean."

He straightened out his knees and fumbled in his pockets until he found a match. He lighted it, and grew tense as the flame sputtered and ran along the match stick. Then he relaxed and held the match close to the brown flesh of the dead Moslem.

"You remember the color of Asfar's skin, Rod?" he asked.

Carson hesitated, looked closer.

"Yes," he said, "but it was nothing like that. His skin was brown all right, but this is darker. This is the brown of…." He stopped short—as though he couldn't finish.

"I know," Kildare said. "It is, as we say, roasted to a turn. Asfar's body is the color of a nicely roasted pig, well browned."

Carson couldn't suppress the shudder as the appalling truth struck him.

"But what—what in the name of heaven could cause this?" he demanded.

"I don't know," Kildare said, "except some weird combination of electrical elements."

Suddenly Carson stiffened as his memory flashed back to the deciphering of the tablets.

"Listen," he said, "do you suppose—I remember something. I know what it is now."

"What are you talking about?" Kildare demanded.

"Now and then there was a word or a phrase that I couldn't quite translate clearly," Carson said. "A part that didn't fit in or make sense. In that passage where the tablets mentioned that the workers in this lower room were killed by the wrath of the gods, there was a phrase that said as nearly as I could figure it out 'their bodies were—' I couldn't decipher that last word, but I know now that it must have been 'cooked' or 'roasted.'"

"Jove," Kildare said, leaning over the body again and probing once more. "That's it, Carson, cooked, roasted, browned to a turn. This is the most horrible thing I have ever seen."

The government man rose to his feet.

"I'm going to look into something else over here," he said. THE AIR was fresher and clearer now, and the purple glow had nearly died out.

Kildare was using matches for illumination as they stopped and stared at a heap of wreckage that reminded Carson of waste copper and brass parts in a junk yard. There was no describing the wreckage, except for the fact that there were broken parts of crude wheels and strange-shaped objects for cylinders with the sides caved in. Each cylinder measured two or three feet across, and there were strips of copper covered with a thick, gummy substance not unlike crude rubber as it comes from the tree.

Kildare led the way around the heap of dull, yellow metal and tossed his nearly burned match over into a black void just ahead of them. The flame glimmered and went out. Then there was a sizzling sound as though the match had struck some extinguishing agent.

Quickly, Kildare lighted two more matches and bent closer. To Carson's amazement, he saw that they were on the brink of an underground stream that flowed smoothly and noiselessly from an opening in a rock. Its course went to the right, across an open space perhaps five by ten feet, then disappeared beneath the rocks at the other end.

There were crude fastenings embedded in the rock floor.

"Those tablets were right," Kildare said hoarsely. "There was a type of electricity discovered, and there was a generator here that supplied the hanging gardens with light. The generator was turned by a water wheel that has been running—"

Suddenly he stopped and frowned.

"Hell, do you suppose that has been running for—" He shook his head. "No, that's impossible. Asfar must have found some way of starting it when he came down here. But evidently the electricity in Asfar's flashlight and that generated here didn't jibe so well. A strange phenomenon took place, a battle of electrical units or something of that kind and Asfar was roasted to death. In the same manner, I suppose, as all those attendants died during an electrical storm."

Kildare turned and went back to the other side of the heap of crushed, broken metal.

"But what I can't figure out," Carson said, "is why this thing was broken up. Who did it? Do you suppose it exploded when Asfar was killed?"

Suddenly, Kildare stopped and backed up a pace. He lighted more matches, bent down, and held them to the floor.

"Look here," he said. "Here's the answer."

Carson stared down at a hammer, a heavy sledge affair with a wooden handle of modern make.

"That's what did it," Kildare explained. "Those two Englishmen. They got down here ahead of us and—" again his voice stopped and he lighted more matches.

"Jove," the government man breathed. "Those two Englishmen were down here. They made drawings of this ancient type of generator and then they smashed the crude machine to bits so that no one else would discover the secret."

"But the drawings!" Carson cried. "How do you know?"

"Look here," Kildare said, pointing beyond the sledge hammer. "There's a pair of calipers, used for taking exact measurements of parts of machinery. And here's a draftsman's compass and a hard pencil."

He moved a little farther away, scrutinizing the floor carefully.

"Here's a small pocket rule such as draftsmen use on an

outside job," he said. "I don't know yet what powers these two Britishers represent but they arranged ahead of time for your exploration to be cut short. That's why our American consul couldn't get anything out of the representative of the British government. These British powers wanted to be there first. When they were attacked by Wu Fang's agents who came in from above, they dropped their draftsmen's tools, smashed the machinery, and rushed upstairs where the beasts and the agents attacked them."

"But how could they come down here with flashlights and not be killed as Asfar was?" Carson demanded.

"I don't know," Kildare said, "but I'm taking it for granted that they were electrical engineers, and in that case they probably suspected something of that sort and used torches or matches. At any rate, we know that they weren't killed in the same way Asfar met his doom. Come on, we've got to find out something and we've got to do it quick. Too much time has been lost already. This is one of the most terrible things I have ever encountered. Get a good breath of air and hang on. Let's go."

Kildare was moving swiftly up those stone steps and Carson was right behind him as they squeezed through into the upper room. The government man moved over to the side near the entrance from above. Then he stopped short, stared about, lighting matches frantically. He nodded shortly.

"Yes," he said, "they're all here. Those agents of Wu Fang that you and I killed. Of course, we didn't get all of them. And there's that big Englishman who was killed by the beasts. He's lying right there beside the stone chest where he fell. But the other one—"

Suddenly, Kildare spun around as he exclaimed, "Why, he fell right here. I'm sure of it. I was positive that my blow on the head knocked him out."

"He's gone?" Carson gasped.

"Yes," Kildare nodded, "and what I want to know is, did they keep their drawings of that generator?"

CHAPTER 7
DEATH AT THE MISSION

"TAKE A long breath," Kildare advised. "We're going up out of here."

In less than a minute they were out in the open air. With a feeling of relief, they filled their lungs again and again with the pure fresh air as they stared about in the darkness.

"Do you suppose that it's the same night as when we had the fight in there?" Carson asked.

"I don't know," Kildare admitted, "but I doubt it. My stomach feels much more empty than that."

There was no sign of the car that had brought them to the mound, nor of the bodies of the dead native soldiers about the place.

"Looks like we'll have to walk," Kildare said. He strode off down the sandy trail by which they had come. For an hour they walked until they reached the main highway from Kerebella to Bagdad. Then, after a few minutes rest, they started on again.

"This thing has got to be stopped," Kildare was repeating over and over again.

"It's getting daylight," he continued. "We've got to call on the government to help. We must impress on the minds of the British that no matter what influential power is tampering with this, it's the most deadly thing the world has ever seen. Why, do you realize, Carson, that one man knowing the secret of this might be able to kill every living person on earth who used electricity in his home? Don't ask me how. I'm not that much of an electrical engineer but—"

Kildare stopped talking and fell into a thoughtful silence. A moment later, Carson broached something that had been troubling him.

"What I can't figure, Kildare," he said, "is how Asfar's body could be so completely roasted and still his white clothing isn't scorched nor is his hair."

Kildare shook his head again as he said, "Don't ask me to explain too much about this. All I know is what I have seen."

They caught a ride in a dilapidated old car that was on its way to Bagdad. The sun was well up when they finally sputtered into the city and reached their hotel. They went straight to their rooms.

Kildare looked down at his white burnoose that was now soiled and grimy.

"No use masquerading in this garb any longer," he said. "The ones we're after know we're here now, anyway; and I feel a lot more comfortable in my own clothes."

Carson heard him make a call on the telephone, heard him talking to the United States consul there in Bagdad.

"Yes," Kildare was saying, "it's imperative that we talk to you at once. Come over to the hotel and have breakfast with us. Very well. We'll look for you in fifteen minutes."

Kildare changed into his own clothing and they went down to breakfast. The consul's face took on a troubled look as the government man explained to him what had happened.

"That's strange," the consul said, "I heard something this morning from El Jerud. That's a British outpost mission school about twenty miles northeast of Bagdad, you know. A Syrian who drove in early this morning said that usually there was plenty of activity around the school as he passed at that hour. But today, there was no one in sight. I tried to telephone the head of the mission who is a personal acquaintance of mine, but I couldn't get him."

"Perhaps the line is down," Carson ventured.

The consul shook his head.

"No," he said. "I can hear the sound of the bell ringing on the other end of the line, but no one answers."

Suddenly, Carson saw Kildare straighten, grow stiff.

"Listen," the government man said. "How long ago was it that I talked with you about exploring the interior of the hanging gardens?"

The consul frowned thoughtfully.

"Why, let me see," he said. "It was the day before yesterday, I believe. Yes, I am sure of it."

"That makes a lapse of about twenty-four hours time," Kildare observed. "Tell me this. Where do they get their electricity for that mission? You say it's isolated?"

"Yes," the consul nodded. "Quite. I think they have their own generating system. Why, does that mean anything?"

"Mean anything?" Kildare repeated. "Jove, I should think it did. How soon can you drive us to El Jerud?"

The consul thought for a moment.

"It's twenty miles," he said, "and the road isn't very good, but I've got a fairly good car and I think we ought to make it in considerably less than an hour."

THE CONSUL broke off sadly and no one spoke for a long time as the car roared and jolted along the rough road. Not a soul was in sight when they turned into the main building of the mission. A choking sound came from the consul's throat as he pulled on the emergency brake and the car halted in front of the main entrance.

"Perhaps," Kildare suggested, "you'd better let us go in first. We're more accustomed to this sort of thing."

The consul shook his head.

"No," he said, "whatever it is, I can stand it. I'll go in with you."

Kildare led the way up the steps to the front door. He tried to see through the curtains for a second before he touched the knob, but the drapes were too heavy. He pushed in the door a few inches while he peered through the crack into a living room.

"Apparently," he said, "these are the living quarters of the man in charge of the mission."

"Yes," the consul said, "Reverend Hawkins and his wife live here in the center of the main building—"

The consul stopped talking then as Kildare pushed the door open a little wider and they saw the foot of a man extending out into the middle of the room. Almost brutally, Kildare shoved the door wide open. There was a gasp of astonishment from both Carson and the consul.

Beside a large library table in the center of the room the Reverend Hawkins sat on a high-backed chair. At first glance he looked as though he were asleep, for his head was turned slightly in the other direction against the back of the chair.

Mrs. Hawkins sat on the other side of the table, slumped grotesquely forward to one side.

Both corpses were a deep-hued brown, similar to the color of Asfar's flesh when his body had been found. Their faces, necks and hands appeared shiny with the natural grease that had oozed out during the cooking process. The flesh had the appearance of a well-turned pig that had been roasted nicely before a slow fire.

A choked exclamation of horror came from the consul.

"Good Heavens!" he shouted. "I can hardly believe it. Why only two days ago, I visited them here."

"I know," Kildare cut in. "It is a horrible thing, but this is only a mere sample of what will come if—"

The government man moved on toward doors that opened from the living room. He opened one in front of a stairs leading to the second floor and went up. Carson followed close behind.

The minister and his wife sat slumped in death.

"Notice anything strange about the color of the air, Rod!" Kildare asked.

Carson stared about him.

"Why, yes," he said. "Funny I didn't notice it before. It's—it's sort of purple."

"Yes," said Kildare. "The light still lingers." He turned quickly to the consul. "What's the latest hour you can remember when anyone heard from Reverend Hawkins directly?" he asked.

"Yesterday afternoon," the consul said. "Yes, I believe that's right. He called the British storehouse in Bagdad yesterday afternoon and put in an order for provisions. They were delivered to him last evening. I learned that when I checked up on him, after failing to get him on the telephone today."

"Then this must have happened last night," Kildare said.

Kildare led the way into another room which was illuminated by the light that shone in through an open window. That room was occupied. There were two boys perhaps ten and twelve years old respectively lying in a double bed.

"This is where Reverend Hawkins' two sons sleep," the consul explained. "Perhaps—"

He stopped short as he caught sight of them and his mouth dropped open in horrified dismay. The two forms that lay in the bed were brown and shiny and horrible-looking. Their eyes were open in a sort of jellied stare.

Kildare reached up to the light that hung well down over the bed within the boys' reach and turned the switch. There was a muffled click. He tried it again. A sharper click this time.

"God," he exclaimed catching his breath. "You know what

that means?" he demanded. "It means that this electrical power mixture or whatever it is doesn't necessarily affect its victims directly in the light. It kills within a radius of the light. For instance, several people in an apartment would all die, become roasted, or whatever strange phenomenon takes place, with just one or two lights on. I dare say there's no heat to it, but some other electrical action that produces this same result. In this case also, as you can see, the bed clothing isn't scorched and the hair is perfectly normal."

"You mean," demanded the consul, "that Reverend Hawkins' sons were killed as a result of the action of the light downstairs in the living room?"

"Exactly," Kildare nodded.

"But I don't see how—"

"I'm not enough of an engineer to explain it," Kildare interrupted. "Perhaps some day well know. Come on, we've got to capture and destroy the whole devilish mechanism before it goes any farther."

"How about the rest of the mission?" the consul ventured.

"What I want to see is the generators," Kildare said. "Do you know where they are?"

"Yes," the consul said. "We can reach the place by going down through this wing of the mission." He pointed to a door at the far end.

"You lead the way," Kildare suggested.

The consul's legs were wobbling as he opened the door and stepped into the corridor. From there they passed into a dormitory lined on either side by cots. Each bed contained a child.

They ranged from the youngest at the door end to those perhaps fourteen or fifteen years old at the far end.

"This was a mission for orphans primarily," the consul explained.

Each body was brown and greasy and had the same staring, jellied eyes as the other bodies they had seen. Some of the mouths were open, as though there had been screaming at the moment of death.

Carson looked grimly straight ahead. He had had enough of this. They reached the door at the other end of the room and followed the consul down a flight of stairs and out into a little room at the back of the wing.

The consul stopped and stood rigid when he reached the threshold. Kildare pushed him aside quickly and entered. The room contained a farm-type generator for manufacturing electricity. Attached to the other end of the little gasoline motor, that was accustomed to running the regular generator, was a small mass of smashed and hammered copper and brass.

ON THE floor lay the form of a stocky man who was baked brown like the other corpses in the mission. Instantly, Carson recognized him as the other Englishman.

Even Kildare looked rather astonished at this turn of events; this was something wholly unexpected. He turned and picked up an axe from the floor and examined it. Then he pointed to the marks of copper on the head.

"Somebody," he said, "has been in here and smashed this whole thing."

"Yes, but who could it have been?" Carson demanded.

"There's only one possibility," Kildare retorted crisply. "Wu Fang and his agents. I still don't know what was behind these two Englishmen. Some powerful combine, no doubt, who wanted to get control of this thing. Apparently, both the Britishers were electrical engineers."

Suddenly, the government man was going through the pockets of the Britisher's clothing.

"There isn't a thing on him," he announced. "I had hoped that this was the end," he admitted a moment later, "but now I realize it isn't."

"I don't understand it at all," the consul choked.

"Here's my theory on it," Kildare offered. "This stocky Englishman escaped even after I hit him. He had the plan that was drawn there and he wanted to try it out. In some way he knew that this mission was one of the few places in this country that had a private generator, and he knew he could experiment here without killing so many people. But the result when he tried to combine this ancient electricity with that generated here at the mission the result was disastrous.

"Wu Fang's agents must have followed this man here to see how the experiment worked out. They kept at a safe distance until it was over, probably guessing that it would have deadly effects within a certain range."

Suddenly, Kildare stepped to the little gasoline motor that had turned the generator and removed the cap of the gasoline tank. He stuck his finger inside.

"Dry as a bone," he said tersely. "When the motor stopped for lack of fuel, Wu Fang's agents came in, found the plans of this mysterious apparatus, and then to be sure that no one else would discover this secret from this new sample device that the English engineer had hurriedly built, they smashed it with the axe. They've gone and the plans have gone with them."

Kildare paused a moment, listening.

"What's that?" he said.

Those words had no more than left his lips than he was hurrying ahead through the door. Outside, the three stood still and listened.

"I didn't hear anything," Carson said.

"Sssh!" Kildare hissed. "Wait."

Now Carson noticed that Kildare was facing a grove at the front of the house where shrubs grew.

A Chinaman lay there. His neat, Occidental business suit was smeared with blood and dirt. He held up one arm weakly and his lips moved inaudibly. Carson recognized him immediately as the neatly-dressed, well-educated Chinaman who had been on the train with them all the way to Bagdad.

"Listen," he whispered, his voice husky with blood. "Listen, please."

"All right," said Kildare who was kneeling beside him. "Go ahead."

"Singapore," the lips uttered weakly. "I will try to tell you. The papers in London mentioned the strange electricity story in connection with the hanging gardens. I—am an electrical engineer representing the interests—of my company in London. I—was there on business. I read—the article and wired—my company. They gave me orders to—follow up.

"On board the train, I recognized—the two Englishmen who sat behind you. They are electrical—engineers from a British firm. I tried to—follow them but they—got away. I saw the short one coming back from—the hanging gardens, so I went out the next morning and trailed him everywhere. He discovered—that I was trailing him. He—shot me and left me here to die. Head of the mission—came out but found nothing. I became unconscious—for a time. Then when I awoke again—I heard talking in my native tongue. Chinamen. They—mention Wu Fang. I hear them say early this morning—before sunrise, they must—get the plans—to Wu Fang in his—"

The Chinaman ceased his painful, gasping narrative as blood spewed from his mouth and his chest heaved spasmodically. He made a desperate effort to finish.

"In his place—in Singapore," he gasped.

Suddenly, the body of the Chinese electrical engineer relaxed and went limp. His eyelids started to close, but suddenly they stopped half way. Kildare made a hasty examination.

"Dead," he said laconically.

CHAPTER 8
THE VEILED WOMAN

THINGS BEGAN happening almost too rapidly for Rod Carson to record after the death of that Chinese electrical engineer. The consul drove them to the Bagdad airdrome where they boarded a plane for Singapore.

The flight to Singapore, which took nearly two days, was

uneventful. After the usual showing of passports and customs inspection on landing, they turned to call a taxi. All the drivers were bickering to carry Kildare and Carson, but the government man was particular in his choice. He handed over his bag to a brown-skinned Malayan who seemed a little more emphatic about selling himself than the rest. Carson looked at him in astonishment.

"Why choose this one?" he asked.

Kildare smiled.

"Because my dear fellow," he said, "I thought it would be best to take the driver that would be most likely to represent Wu Fang, although I am quite sure we know which one was sent by the yellow devil."

"You think he knows we've come then?" Carson demanded.

Kildare gave a short nod.

"Of course," he said.

He turned and pointed out of the back window of the cab. "See that British driver there," he said. "At least, he looks British."

Carson nodded shortly as he saw a heavy-set, cocky fellow watching them with one foot on his cab.

"That's the driver from Wu Fang," Kildare said. "I'm sure of it. He doesn't act like a cab driver. These cab drivers, especially here in Singapore, have a certain way of advancing toward you, of getting their trade, that that fellow hasn't acquired, although I must admit that he plays his part fairly well."

"But look here," Carson demanded, more bewildered than ever, "you told our driver that you wanted to go to the United States consul in plain hearing of that English fellow."

"Why not?" Kildare shrugged. "After all, being trailed may be the only way in which we will be able to locate Wu Fang."

The cab was gathering more speed as it moved toward the gate of the airdrome, but it had to slow for a turn that brought them out on the main road to the center of Singapore. In fact, they had to stop for a car was coming toward them on the wrong side of the road.

Kildare leaned forward, gripped the front rail in preparation for a crash and Carson braced his feet against the back of the front seat. Then suddenly he leaped forward. That other car, a black sedan, swerved toward them with a squeal of brakes and burning tires. The whole thing was obviously intentional.

The two cars stopped side by side and now Carson's eyes were bulging at a figure in the rear seat of that sedan. It was the figure of a woman whose clothing could not hide the beautiful curves of her body. The woman in the sedan made a quick movement and a white scrap of paper came sailing in through the open window in front of Carson. He tried to catch it but it struck his hand and dropped to the floor. Carson stared at the figure of the girl. His lips parted and he half-uttered a name as the sedan sped away.

"Catch that car!" Kildare shouted to their cab driver. "A pound if you make it!"

The brown-skinned Malayan driver turned, his eyes rolling in astonishment.

"That's right," Kildare affirmed. "A whole pound for yourself. Nearly five dollars in our money. Catch that car and it's yours."

Both Kildare and Carson were leaning forward as the Malayan

shot the car in reverse and backed the car so that he could turn it enough to pull into the road to the left instead of the right as he had originally planned to do. Then, with a final start, the cab got away in pursuit of the big black sedan which was rapidly drawing away from them.

Carson was unwrapping the note that the woman had thrust at him. It was folded around a copper penny to give it sufficient weight to carry through the air. Then he and Kildare read:

GENTLEMEN:

IF YOU STAY IN SINGAPORE FOR ONE HOUR, YOU AND ALL OF THE BETTER CLASS INHABI-TANTS WILL DIE. I AM GIVING YOU THIS CHANCE TO GET OUT WHILE THERE IS STILL TIME.

WU FANG

The two men exchanged glances. Then suddenly, Kildare grabbed Carson's arm.

"Look out!" he cried.

The cab swerved recklessly, for another taxi had come charging up alongside and had swung directly into their path, cutting them off. The Malayan driver had to take to the ditch to keep from smashing into the other car.

Crash!

Kildare and Carson were thrown violently to the side of the cab. As it lurched again, they came to an abrupt stop with the right front corner tilted down.

Kildare fumbled for the latch of the door and swung it open. He leaped out angrily.

"What are you waiting for?" he demanded of the driver. "Is the car damaged?"

"Maybe yes, maybe no."

Carson ran around on the other side of the car and looked at the right front wheel that was sagging. It was in a hole where it had dropped off the shoulder of the road.

"Come on!" Carson cried. "Put her in reverse and we'll help you out of here."

STILL CURSING, the brown-skinned driver did as he was ordered. The wheels spun, the car jolted, and with a grunt, it backed out of the gutter. Kildare and Carson climbed in again.

"You're all right," Kildare said. "Now get going."

Carson was staring far, far down the road in the wake of that other car and he was still holding the note in his right fist.

"Did you see her, Kildare?" he asked.

Kildare nodded.

"You are sure it was Tanya?" he asked.

Carson nodded. His jaw muscles were bulging from the tight clenching of his teeth.

"Yes," he said. "I couldn't see very plainly through her veil, but I am sure it was she. She tossed the note in to me. She's still in Wu Fang's employ."

"No," Kildare cut in quietly, "I think you're wrong about that, Rod. She's still his loyal slave, held to him by some irresistible hypnotic influence that he has cast over her."

Somehow, Carson seemed to feel a sort of exhilaration at the assurance that his suspicion concerning Tanya was not true.

"You are sure of this?" he demanded of Kildare.

"No one is sure of anything with Wu Fang," Kildare said, "but I have some pretty straight information that whatever Wu Fang is, he's not particularly interested in women, except as they further his devilish plans. He may be using these beautiful girls with the idea of developing them to follow in his footsteps—if and when he's gone."

Kildare broke off abruptly and stared down the road.

"Did you notice the driver of that taxi that forced us into the ditch?" he asked, changing the subject.

"Yes," Carson nodded, his eyes still far, far down the road on a mere black speck that was the sedan. "You were right as usual, Kildare. It was the cockney Englishman who you suspected from the first to be Wu Fang's agent. Evidently he has a much faster car than we picked."

They were coming into thicker traffic now. Kildare leaned over and spoke to the driver.

"Never mind trying to catch that car anymore," he said. "Just take us to the American consul."

Kildare looked at the note again, taking it from Carson's fingers.

Something was happening to Carson, something that he couldn't explain. This girl Tanya was so lovely, so fair. She seemed so delicate, so fine to be doing the dirty work of a yellow fiend like Wu Fang. It was like using a gold spade to shovel filth out of the streets.

Carson heard Kildare exclaim, "An hour! An hour to get out of Singapore or everyone dies."

Carson frowned. There were a great many things about this

government man that he couldn't understand. Kildare was looking out of the window and up at the dusky sky. He glanced at his watch and shook his head.

"Lord!" he muttered. "Do you know what that means, Rod? It means that Wu Fang has established his generators here in Singapore. His agents reached here before we did and set up their apparatus. So you know what's going to happen within an hour?"

Carson shook his head uncertainly.

"If you and I don't get out of town, we're all going to die," he said. "At least, that's how I figure it."

"That isn't what I mean," Kildare said. "In three quarters of an hour, every electric light in Singapore that is accustomed to being turned on at this hour will be burning."

"Good Lord!" Carson exploded suddenly. "You mean he's going to try to kill everyone in Singapore as it happened at the mission?"

"Exactly," Kildare nodded, "unless, that is, we get out of town."

"What are you going to do?" Carson demanded. "If I had my way about it, we'd stay here and fight."

"Yes," Kildare agreed, "that's our plan. I've got one more ace in the hole, though, and I'm going to spring it the minute we reach the American consul's home."

As he spoke, the car drew up to the curb.

"Here we are now," Kildare said.

They got out before a neat, two-story stucco house with a small garden and lawn about it. The consul, a small, alert man, had apparently been expecting them.

"You received our message, consul?" Kildare asked after brief introductions were made.

"Yes," the consul nodded. "I turned the matter over to the police and I've kept in touch with them ever since I received the wire from Bagdad."

"I see," Kildare said slowly, while he studied the Singapore consul carefully. "But as yet, nothing has turned up. You haven't found a trace of Wu Fang?"

The consul's eyes widened a little in surprise.

"You seem to expect it, Mr. Kildare," he said.

"Quite," Kildare admitted. "But we have something much more important at the moment to be taken care of. You would, perhaps, have some influence with the electric light and power company that furnishes the electricity for the city of Singapore?"

The consul hesitated.

"Why, yes," he said, "I have met the president of the company. He would probably grant me a small favor, if it wasn't asking too much."

"It will be asking a lot," Kildare said crisply. "The point is this. The lights can't go on in Singapore tonight or any other night, until we get this menace cleared up."

He told the consul of the menace, of the death that awaited the residents of Singapore if they turned on their electric lights.

He finished with, "Now, will you call him at once?"

The consul lighted a cigarette nervously; Kildare's words had begun to take effect. He reached for the phone. Two or three minutes elapsed, then he was talking to the president of the power and light company of Singapore, explaining as best he could the reasons for his request.

"No, no!" Carson heard him say. "I tell you it's not fantastic. It's—"

"Let me have that phone, please," Kildare cut in, reaching for the instrument. The government man talked to the power magnate, but in vain.

"All right, die with the rest of them," he finished as the other continued to protest.

Kildare slammed the receiver back on the hook, glanced at his watch and whirled around to the city consul.

"We've got to get the Governor-General to issue an order," he said. "You must know him well enough so that he will believe you."

"Yes," said the consul. "Yes, indeed. I believe I can arrange it. I hadn't thought of that."

He went to the phone, got the number, and began talking rapidly.

"You see," he finished, "it may be only temporary, Governor, but I have enough confidence in my friend to feel that he knows what he's talking about. Yes, sir. We'll notify you at once when things are cleared up so that the power and lights can go on again. Thank you, sir."

He hung up the receiver and took a long, relieved breath.

"There," he said, "that's that. Thank heaven, he's going to push through an order to turn off all the electricity in the city."

"ALL RIGHT," Kildare said, stepping forward. "Let's have that phone. I want to call the three principal newspapers in

Singapore. They'll want to know, immediately, what the reason is for turning off the electricity. I've got a good story cooked up for them."

One after another, Kildare called the editorial offices of the various newspapers and in each case he advised them to send over a reporter to the home of the American consul.

"You really are going to give them the whole story?" the consul asked.

Kildare nodded.

"I'm going to give them the whole story and more," he said.

"More?" Carson said. "Are you going to build up a story for them?"

"You'll see," Kildare smiled. "It's a long chance but I believe it will work."

He walked the length of the living room and back. A moment later, the doorbell rang and the servant announced a reporter from one of the papers. A few moments later, two more arrived. One was a smiling, intelligent-looking Chinaman; the other two were Britishers.

"I have called you," Kildare said, "to—"

He stopped suddenly as the street lamps outside went out. No lights had been turned on in the house as yet, but they could see each other without difficulty. Kildare nodded toward the street lights that had just been extinguished.

"Perhaps you are wondering why that light went out," he said.

The Chinaman smiled.

"Maybe bulb burn out," he suggested.

Kildare shook his head and walked over to the window.

"Come here," he said to the newspaper men. "Do you see any lights anywhere on the streets or in any of the offices?"

Carson saw the astonishment written on the reporters' faces. Kildare was quite obviously enjoying the show.

"Now I will tell you about it," he said.

The reporters returned to their chairs and waited expectantly. Kildare sat on the edge of the table and puffed leisurely at a cigar as he told them the whole story of the strange electricity from the hanging gardens of Babylon.

"You see," he said, "we happen to know that Wu Fang, the yellow devil who menaces the world, is preparing to kill every inhabitant in the city by combining this strange type of electricity with the current already used."

The government man leaned forward and spoke in a low whisper.

"But this is one time when the law is going to be one jump ahead of the Dragon Lord of Crime," he said. "Mr. Cameron, the head of the electrical plant here in Singapore, has just phoned me that he has developed what might be called an antidote for this strange electrical combination. It works in this way: when the ancient type generator is attached near the power house, the people who are installing it will be killed immediately by the backlash."

Kildare's explanation was cut off by a cry from one of the reporters.

"Can we print that, please?" the Chinaman asked eagerly.

"Yes, do we dare print that just as you told it to us?" one of the Britishers demanded excitedly.

Kildare nodded amiably.

"Yes, gentlemen," he said. "If you think it would do any good, go ahead. And now I believe that is all I have for you. How soon will that be out on the street?"

"They're holding the papers now," one reporter said. "We'll smear it all over the front page," the other Britisher told him.

"You may depend upon it that they will begin selling my paper on this article in about an hour, Mr. Kildare," the Chinese reporter said.

"Very well," Kildare nodded.

Carson and the consul stared at Kildare in bewilderment after the three reporters had left.

"Listen, Kildare," Carson begged. "Tell me straight. Is that story true that you gave them?" Kildare smiled.

"You mean about the antidote current that Cameron phoned me about? No, of course not. I was afraid they would see through the thing."

"But look here," the consul cut in, "what's the object of stringing them along on something that isn't true? That story will be in all the principal newspapers of the city."

"Exactly," Kildare said. "Wait a minute. I've got to put in a call."

He lifted the receiver and said, "Give me the police head-quarters at once. Yes, that's right."

When someone answered on the other end of the line, he said, "This is Val Kildare of the United States Government

Service. I'm calling from the home of the American consul. Get a pencil and paper, please. I'd like to have you jot down something. I've an unusual request to make.

"I'd like you to send me a man. Height, six feet one. Weight, one hundred and sixty-five pounds. Long, thin face. Light hair. Have you someone down there that answers that general description? No, not a prisoner, one of the police officers—All right, I'll hang on."

Several seconds passed. Then Kildare was speaking again.

"You have? That's fine. Will you send him up at once?—Fine. I'll be waiting."

"For heaven's sake, Kildare," Carson demanded, "what are you doing? You'll have me crazy trying to figure out your moves before you explain them."

"It is a bit complicated when you don't know what it's all about," Kildare admitted. "Look here. We have the lights turned off now. What is our next move?"

"To get Wu Fang," Carson exploded.

"Exactly," Kildare nodded. "That's what I'm trying to do."

"But how in the name of—" Carson began.

"Well, how would you go about finding him?" Kildare challenged.

"That's what I mean," Carson said. "The police here haven't been able to ferret out his location. But what's that got to do with the—"

"Listen," Kildare explained. "Within an hour Wu Fang will be reading the glaring headlines in the papers explaining why the lights in Singapore were turned off and who was responsible."

"Yes," the consul cut in, "but he will also find out where you and Carson are and that you're going to the residence of Mr. Archibald Cameron."

"Our call on Mr. Cameron," Kildare explained further, "is merely a blind. Or rather, I should say, your call, Rod. You and a man who is coming up from headquarters will call on him after we give Wu Fang a chance to send his agents up there to spy on you."

"You don't mean to tell me that we're already being watched, do you?" Carson demanded.

"Certainly we're being watched," Kildare said, "but whatever agents he has on our trail now are merely to prevent our getting away."

"Wu Fang is probably feeling pretty elated about this thing in spite of the fact that we have turned the lights off on him. He knows that eventually they will go on again because people won't stop using electricity simply because there's a mad yellow beast loose somewhere on the earth who might hook up on his own generators with their dynamos and kill them. All he has to do is to wait until the electricity is turned on again.

"But now he has this counter menace that I have cooked up to worry about. Cameron is supposed to know about it. When Wu Fang hears of this, he will naturally suspect that it's a stall on my part and he'll send agents up to Cameron's house to see if there's any truth in it.

"You, Rod, are going to Cameron's house. The man that is

being sent up from headquarters will go as me, dressed in my clothing and made up a bit to look more like me."

"And what will you do?" Carson asked.

"Can't you guess," Kildare smiled. "I'll be there trailing Wu Fang's agents who in turn will be trailing yon. The police have tried in vain to find Wu Fang. Apparently he has a very well hidden hideout, so the only way we can reach him is to follow one of his agents directly back to him."

"What are we supposed to do while you're trailing Wu Fang's agents?" Carson demanded. "Spend the night at Cameron's?"

"We'll figure that out later," Kildare told him.

The bell in the front hall jangled.

"There's the man from headquarters now," Kildare said.

CHAPTER 9
FACES IN THE NIGHT

VAL KILDARE stepped into the hall ahead of the servant and opened the door. Carson peered out into the hall at the man who was to accompany him to Cameron's house in the disguise of Kildare. He was astonished to see the remarkable resemblance of this newcomer to the government man.

"Permit me to introduce myself," the newcomer said. "I am Sir Reginald Owen, Chief Inspector of the Singapore Police."

Kildare smiled pleasantly.

"I am Val Kildare," he said, "and this is certainly a surprise, Sir Reginald. I have heard much about you of course, but I didn't expect that you would come yourself to impersonate me."

The two men, alike as two peas in the same pod except for their facial features, entered the spacious living room of the consul's home.

"Permit me," Kildare said, "to introduce Sir Reginald Owen. I presume you know him, Consul."

The American consul nodded and smiled.

"And my friend, Rod Carson," Kildare added. "Perhaps you have heard of him. He has done a neat bit of exploring in archaeological work."

"Oh, yes, of course," Sir Reginald nodded, taking Carson's hand in a cordial grasp.

Then the face of the Britisher became perplexed again as he turned to Kildare and said, "I don't quite understand this impersonation plan. What is it all about?"

"I confess, Sir Reginald," Kildare said, "you have me rather at my wits' ends. You see, here's the general idea. I have arranged things so that Wu Fang will know that in another hour and a half, let us say, we will be going, Carson and myself, to the home of Mr. Archibald Cameron. Wu Fang will think this is a mission that will spell doom to him and destruction to his plans. I devised this scheme simply to be sure that his agents will be there. I'm certain they will be agents who will report back to the yellow devil immediately."

"I see," Sir Reginald nodded quickly. "Yes, of course. And you plan to follow the agents of Wu Fang to learn his whereabouts."

"That's is," Kildare admitted, "but in order that there will be no slip-up, I asked headquarters to send me a man corresponding to my general description. I thought of course they would send up some patrolman. I never dreamed they would send you, Sir Reginald, the head of the whole police force."

The Britisher laughed, apparently enjoying the joke as much as anyone.

"You'll go through with it?" Kildare asked.

"Certainly. Delighted. May need a touch of grease paint here and there to make me resemble you more closely, though. I think I could get into that tweed suit of yours, Kildare."

The government man nodded.

"Thanks for your cooperation," he said.

There was an exchange of clothing and then by the flickering light of the candles, Kildare altered his face so that he looked quite unlike the Kildare that Wu Fang and his agents knew. He turned to Sir Reginald Owen, who now looked more like Kildare than the government man did himself.

"You know the way to Mr. Archibald Cameron's house, Sir Reginald?" he asked.

"Yes, of course," nodded the Britisher. "It's not far from here."

"Good," Kildare nodded. "And if I might make a suggestion, I think it would be a good idea to walk. It would be better also, I believe, to wait a few minutes until our time is up."

Carson watched the clock while they waited. Kildare was busy writing something on a piece of paper. When he had finished, he handed it to Carson.

"There," he said, "I think that will cover it, Rod. Just hand that to Archibald Cameron. If he's got any sense at all, he'll take his cue and do his part. Read it if you want to know what it's all about."

Carson did read it. He saw on the paper:

UPON RECEIVING THE TWO GUESTS, YOU WILL BE HANDED THIS NOTE. READ IT CAREFULLY. IT IS BEST THAT YOU DO EXACTLY AS IT ORDERS. THIS IS WHAT YOU ARE TO DO. FIRST, COMPLAIN ABOUT THE HEAT AND ORDER YOUR SERVANTS TO OPEN SEVERAL WINDOWS.

AS THEY DO SO, YOU WILL SAY IN A LOUD VOICE, "YES, OF COURSE, THERE ARE A NUMBER OF PEOPLE WHO KNOW ABOUT THIS. THERE IS THE INVENTOR—OF COURSE I CAN NOT DIVULGE HIS NAME, SEVERAL OF OUR ENGINEERS, AND A NUMBER OF PEOPLE ON OUR OPERATING STAFF. SO YOU SEE, IT WOULD BE QUITE DIFFICULT FOR WU FANG TO PUT A STOP TO THIS BY KILLING ME, OR EVEN ONE OR TWO OF THE OTHER MEN INVOLVED."

AFTER THE WINDOWS HAVE BEEN OPENED, GO TO THE NEAREST ONE AND DRAW THE SHADES, BEING SURE, HOWEVER, TO LEAVE ENOUGH OPENING SO THAT THE CONVERSATION MAY BE PLAINLY HEARD. YOU ARE TO TALK GENERALLY ABOUT A NEW INVENTION THAT NEUTRALIZES A MIXTURE OF CURRENTS AND HAS A DEADLY EFFECT UPON THOSE OPERATING THE

MENACING NEW CURRENT. GIVE THE IMPRESSION AT ALL TIMES THAT YOU UNDERSTAND THIS FREQUENCY OF A THIRD DIMENSION COMPLETELY—THAT IT ISN'T ANYTHING NEW TO YOU, AS WU FANG THINKS.

AFTER YOU HAVE TALKED FOR TEN MINUTES ON THIS SUBJECT, YOUR SERVANT WILL CALL YOU INTO THE OTHER ROOM WHERE DRINKS WILL BE SERVED. THERE THE WINDOWS WILL BE TIGHTLY LOCKED AND SHUTTERED. YOU MUST BE READY TO ACT QUICKLY IF YOU ARE NEEDED. DO NOT BE SURPRISED AT ANYTHING YOU HEAR. REMEMBER, YOU AND YOUR OFFICE ARE BEING WATCHED CONSTANTLY BY WU FANG AND HIS AGENTS.

"Looks as though it ought to do the trick," Carson said as he finished reading.

Kildare took the note from him and handed it to Sir Reginald.

"Would you mind glancing over that and then signing it, just to make it a little more authoritative?"

Sir Reginald's silver gray eyes widened as he read the note.

"By Jove," he said, "this is clever. Deucedly clever. Of course I'll sign it. And you will be outside?"

"I'll be outside trailing Wu Fang's agents," Kildare said. "I may need help. If I do, I'll let you know."

"But, how?" Carson demanded.

"I'll figure that out later," Kildare said. He glanced at his watch. "I think you two should start now," he said. "I'll be trailing along directly."

Carson and Sir Reginald turned and shook hands with the consul. As the door closed quickly behind them, they were suddenly enveloped in pitch blackness.

Now Carson realized that Kildare had been right. He could hear no suspicious sounds behind him, but he could feel intuitively that there was someone trailing him.

THEY WALKED on and soon heard a boy yelling something—in three different languages. First he said it in English, then in French, and last, in German. It all meant the same thing; he was selling papers that told all about the lights going out in Singapore—the papers with the big front-page story that Kildare had given the reporters.

They walked on briskly for another block and now Sir Reginald was squinting at the dark houses on their right. All of them were fine residences, set far back, with elaborately shrubbed lawns. At the corner, he turned and approached one.

Now and then Carson glanced back and stared behind him. Once or twice he saw a moving shadow in the darkness, but that was all. Still, he knew they were there, those watchers sent by Wu Fang, trailing them with orders not to strike this time, but merely to get certain information for their master.

Sir Reginald rang the doorbell of the great house and a servant opened the door. Sir Reginald slipped his foot in the opening and stepped inside quickly. The butler was astonished.

"There's no harm going to be done," Sir Reginald said quickly.

Carson saw a hideous face at the window.

"It is imperative that we see your master at once. Tell him there's a message here from Sir Reginald Owen."

The face of the butler was white and bewildered as he bowed and backed away.

"Yes, sir," he stammered. "Yes, indeed. A messenger from Sir Reginald Owen."

The butler left hurriedly. Almost immediately, a gray-haired, distinguished-looking gentleman came forth from one of the doors at the side of the great reception hall. He looked blankly from one to the other.

"Am I to understand that you bring me a message from Sir Reginald Owen?" he demanded.

"Yes," Carson said, stepping forward. "I have it."

He handed Cameron the message of explanation that Kildare had written. The power magnate took it and scanned it rapidly. His brow furrowed.

"What is all this?" he demanded.

"It is in regard to the turning off of the lights in Singapore at the command of the governor-general." Sir Reginald said.

"It was a ridiculous move," Cameron snapped out. "I don't know who this fellow Kildare thinks he is, coming in here and running things. Perhaps one of you is Kildare."

Sir Reginald spoke up.

"Yes," he said, "I am Kildare. But let me assure you that—"

"You don't sound like an American," Cameron cut in suspiciously.

Sir Reginald came closer to the power magnate.

"Permit me to explain one thing," he said quietly in a low, steely voice. "Mr. Kildare knows exactly what he's doing."

"You have a good opinion of yourself," Cameron said. "There's something funny going on here. If Kildare is an American, you're not he. You talk like an Englishman."

"Very well," Sir Reginald said in a low, commanding tone. "You have guessed correctly. I am not Val Kildare. I am Sir Reginald Owen, commissioner of police here in Singapore. If there's any doubt in your mind now about your course of procedure, Cameron, may I say, that you are hereby ordered by the commissioner of police to do exactly as Kildare requires in the note."

"But what's Kildare got to do with this?" Cameron demanded, glancing at the note again.

"The plan is Kildare's," Sir Reginald explained. "I merely signed it. Now read the note carefully and proceed along those lines."

That little speech had caused a complete change in Archibald Cameron's attitude. He studied the orders from Kildare, and after reading them over twice, he nodded.

"I think I have it," he said.

Cameron turned abruptly and led the way into a large living room.

"Come in, gentlemen," he said. "I am glad to see you. We'll talk this thing over and see what arrangements we can make. Oh, Baskings!"

"Yes, sir," the butler answered. "Did you call, sir?"

"Yes," Cameron nodded. "Open the window. It's stuffy in here."

"Yes, sir, at once, sir."

The drapes were pulled back and the windows were opened.

Cameron, taking his cue again from the note said in a loud voice, "As I was saying, Kildare, Wu Fang wouldn't gain anything by killing me. You see, there are quite a number of people who know about this reversing machine. Killing me would gain Wu Fang nothing but a lot of trouble. There are several people on my staff who know the secret of this. And besides that, the formula and drawings of the apparatus that will combat this devilish new circuit are recorded in several of our offices."

He went on and on, following Kildare's orders. A breeze blew the curtains wide, nickering the candles that were the only illumination in the house.

Carson shot a glance at the window when that happened and saw a face. It was only there for an instant, but that was long enough for him to see it plainly. It was a yellow face, slant-eyed and flat-nosed.

With an effort, Carson restrained himself from grabbing his gun and leaping to his feet for that would have ruined everything. Instead, with calm deliberation, he shifted his eyes deliberately back to the face of the power magnate who was going on with his talk. As the curtains blew in a second time, Cameron saw another face, an awful, brown thing that vanished the instant after it came into plain view.

HE FELT almost like cheering and yelling, "Swell! Everything's fine! They fell right into your trap, Kildare."

The government man, of course, must be out there watching and trailing.

"What do you say we have a whiskey and soda?" Cameron suggested, rising.

As the butler entered, he stood stock still for a moment at the door. Carson saw him staring past them toward the window on his right. Basking's face suddenly went white and frightened.

"I say, sir—" he began.

"Baskings," Cameron cut in. "Serve us with whiskey and soda in the library. I have some curios to show you gentlemen."

"We would be more than glad to see them," Cameron said.

"But I say, sir," the butler cried, still staring past them at the open window. "I—" He raised a trembling finger toward that window.

"Did you hear what I said?" Archibald Cameron snapped angrily. "Whiskey and soda served in the library at once."

"Yes, sir," the man said, turning.

In the hall, Carson said to Cameron, "Your butler saw the same thing I did."

Cameron eyed the young explorer sharply as he demanded, "What do you mean?"

"Faces at the window," Carson whispered. "Two of them, a hideous Chinese face and a Malayan."

The power magnate's face was white now.

"Is there any danger?" he asked anxiously. "Will they attack?" Carson shook his head.

"No," he said. "Not a chance. They've been sent here to watch and listen. Very shortly, they will be going back to Wu Fang.

While you are in the library, I think it would be best if you raised your voice particularly loud."

When they entered the library, Carson walked over to the locked and shuttered windows and opened a transom above one of them.

Then Cameron lifted his voice again loudly as he continued, "As I was saying, gentlemen, we have nothing to fear from this yellow fiend, Wu Fang. We have the lights turned off now in Singapore, but very shortly they will go on again. They were not turned off, as the papers said, to save Singapore but to give my engineers a chance to hook on their saving device. You may rest assured that when these lights are turned on again, Wu Fang, or whoever is behind this, will die a most horrible death."

Carson heard a slight scraping outside the end window in the library. It sounded as though someone were climbing up on the outside. Cameron hesitated for a moment but Carson leaped toward him and nodded encouragingly.

"Keep talking," he hissed. "That's the stuff. Ramble on." Then in his normal voice, the young explorer continued, "But Mr. Cameron, let me ask you this question. Is it possible for all other power companies to use the same system to defeat the plans of this yellow devil Wu Fang?"

Cameron opened his mouth to speak, but stopped short as a sound came to him from across the hall. A door leading from the living room had been closed.

Carson whirled around, his eyes glued upon the door of the living room. At the same time he touched Cameron and hissed out of the corner of his mouth, "Keep talking."

The power magnate did the best he could, answering Carson's questions in that same loud voice that was a little shaky now. Carson was watching the knob on the door. It was turning over so slowly and the door was opening inch by inch.

CHAPTER 10
THE PHANTOM DOCK

EVERY EYE was upon that opening door. Carson wondered if someone had been hiding in that room when they were in there, then he remembered that one of the windows was open. This, then, would be one of the agents of Wu Fang, perhaps that flat-nosed, yellow fiend of whom he had caught a glimpse through the window.

Suddenly a face appeared in the shadow near the door. Carson recognized it instantly as the disguised countenance of Kildare.

The moment Kildare saw that the curtains were drawn in the library across the hall, he opened the door to its full width and walked on tip-toe toward them. He pointed to Archibald Cameron.

"Keep talking," he hissed.

Although it was evident that the effort was great, Cameron did his best. Kildare glanced at the three windows again, more minutely this time. He took Carson and Sir Reginald a little distance away.

"Listen," he whispered with his lips close to the ears of both. "There are three of them. I think Wu Fang sent three so that they could split up in case they were followed. It will take the three of us to trail them. We can't slip up. Come on. I'll follow you."

"Where are they now?" Sir Reginald asked.

"I followed the three of them," Kildare whispered, "to the three windows of the library. There are two Chinamen and a Malayan. You take the Malayan, if you will, Sir Reginald. Carson and I will tackle the two yellow beasts."

They tip-toed across the hall into the living room.

"You came in this way?" Sir Reginald asked.

"Yes," Kildare whispered, "through one of the open windows."

Sir Reginald and Carson followed Kildare out of the largest of the windows.

"Now," Kildare ordered when they were out on the veranda, "not another sound. Keep your hand on me, Sir Reginald. Carson, you follow Sir Reginald by touch and I'll lead you to the spot."

They crept softly around the back of the house. It was apparent that Kildare had trod this ground before and knew exactly where he was going. Suddenly he stopped and Sir Reginald and Carson came to a halt behind him.

That scraping sound was coming again, and against the dim light that filtered through the curtains of the library window, they could make out several figures. Near the center window of the library, they saw a figure clinging to the wall, stretched out like a bat.

Kildare whispered something to Sir Reginald and then put his lips close to Carson's ear as he said. "That's the Malayan there. Sir Reginald will take care of him. You and I will follow the two Chinamen."

The scraping sound from the Malayan gave evidence that he was coming down. They could see him lowering himself along the wall.

As the Burmese dropped to the ground with a light thud that was scarcely audible to them a few feet away, Sir Reginald moved forward.

"There he goes, Sir Reginald," Kildare said.

At the same time, the figure, moving as silently and swiftly as a panther, crept off to the right in the darkness. As silently as that brown-skinned Malayan had slipped into the shadows, so Sir Reginald Owen moved off.

After a mumbled consultation the two remaining forms parted, one going to the right along the edge of the house and the other to the left.

At that instant, Carson felt Kildare give him a quick shove toward the front of the house and he heard the government man say, "Good luck, Rod."

As Carson started off on his mission, he realized that Kildare had given him the easier job, for the other Chinaman had started out through the rear yard over fences. The young explorer's chase led on and on through crowded streets where he nearly lost sight of the yellow beast he was trailing. They progressed through less thickly populated sections until they came near the Chinese quarter. Anything was liable to happen from now on; any moment now this yellow shadow before Carson would dive into a hole in the wall and vanish into one of the entrances to the secret hiding place of Wu Fang.

But the fellow went on and on, with apparently no inkling that he was being followed. Carson trailed him until they reached an alley in a smelly, narrow winding street of the yellow quarter. Without the slightest hesitation, the squat agent turned into the alley.

Carson slipped down into the black passage. He still couldn't see a thing, but he could hear a sound of bare feet running up a flight of stairs with perfect abandon. No, this agent of Wu Fang was making no attempt to hide his presence or his movements.

Carson groped hurriedly along the wall and his feet stumbled against the bottom of a stairs as he heard a door open above. The door creaked eerily on rusty hinges.

His short stay this time in Singapore hadn't given Rod Carson much time to explore the city, but on previous visits, he had become quite well acquainted with the various sections. He realized now that they were getting over very close to the wharfs and the dock area. If the scum of humanity ever collected anywhere, it was here in the waterfront of Singapore.

Carson was going up the stairs as fast as he could, making much less noise in his ascension than the Chinaman had. What about that door at the top? Would that be open?

He heard a door close quickly, but there was no sound of a key turning. Carson realized, as he ran up the steps, that he must not catch up with this fellow but he must be near enough to follow him accurately.

Carson reached the door, turned the knob and pushed the door in without any trouble. He stepped inside and stopped to listen. If he had thought things were black outside, but in here it was as though he had been plunged into a bottle of thick ink.

There was the stench of an old, rotted building about the place. The floor seemed to sag under his feet as though the boards were going to give away at any moment.

A sound came from ahead and to the left. A gentle pad, pad, pad of feet—a creak of a board. Carson realized that he must be careful not to strike that board himself. He began groping his way along.

Suddenly the sound of the other stopped, and Carson became motionless. There was nothing but utter silence!

Seconds clicked by—dragged on like hours, then a sound relieved that awful tension and Carson dared take a breath again.

Creak!

Was that another door opening on rusty hinges? No, there it was again.

Creak!

THERE WAS a very gentle thud followed by silence. Carson crept forward, stopped as he heard a muffled scraping. A creak sounded again, followed by a thud as though an object had dropped from a few feet to a floor below.

Carson couldn't figure the thing out. Perhaps this beast had opened a trap door and dropped down through it. That might account for the squeak of a pulley, but where was the trap door and where was the opening? He must find it.

He thought he saw a blotch of light ahead of him and groped toward it. Yes, there was a window on that side of the room and it was open.

He realized now that the creaking he had heard had been the slow opening of the window by the Oriental and the thud had been the weight dangling at the bottom.

Hurriedly, Carson stuck his head out of the window and looked about He heard the padding of feet again, although it came from quite a distance away. From the window, he looked directly down into a yard and saw that there was a building directly behind this one. It was a one-story affair with a flat roof.

Then suddenly, Carson leaned farther out as he spotted a figure crouched over and moving at the other end of that long, shed-like roof. That was the answer then. The creak of timber had come when this yellow man had leaped from the window ledge to the roof across the alley.

Carson tried to judge the distance. Could he make that in a jump? He would have to try.

Carson gathered all his strength and leaped out into the air. His toe barely touched the edge of the flat roof and slipped off. He was going down, but he flung his hands out desperately and caught the edge of the roof just as he was about to drop into the alley. He managed to pull himself up quickly, swung one leg over and rolled his body on to the roof. In the next instant, he was up and dashing across the roof, making as little noise as he could.

The young explorer saw a movement below him as he lay on

the edge of the roof and stared down. There was water there below. Why, this was the roof of a small wharf. He heard the splashing of oars, but apparently, the yellow man had come to the point where he wanted to take no chance on being heard, for the splashing ceased and only the slow dip of the oars was heard.

As Carson stared about, he saw lights on several ships. They were certainly on the edge of a wharf, but how had that yellow beast gotten down? He saw the boat now as it pulled away from the wharf. There was no other boat in sight, but he must follow that man!

Carson began feeling about under him, but there was nothing there. He stopped suddenly as his hand came into contact with a spike at the comer of the building. That was it! A spike, and perhaps another one down farther. At least he could hang from the first spike and drop into the water without making too much noise.

Carson lowered himself over the edge, felt around with his feet and found another spike. He slid down along the corner of the wharf and stepped on the second spike. He saw that Wu Fang's agent had taken the only boat there.

Carson shrugged. All right, he would have to swim for it. The water should be warm and also, he remembered with a sickly feeling, shark-infested.

With a determined shake of his head, Carson removed his coat and rolled it into a bundle. Being sure that his automatic and his flashlight were at the top of the bundle, he tied it to the back of his head, using the sleeves to bind it under his chin.

That done, he slipped into the water and struck out in a strong breast stroke in the wake of the rowboat that the Chinaman had taken.

In a few minutes of swimming, he was almost directly behind it and gaining all the time. Soon, the oarsman pulled on his left oar, turning the small craft sharply toward the shore.

Carson stared ahead of the boat at the black wall there. From what he could see in the darkness, there appeared to be a solid stone barrier in front of the boat, the end of a great pier that jotted out in the harbor.

Why was that boat heading for that impassable wall? The Chinaman would bump the nose of the boat directly into it! Carson swam a little closer, then suddenly he stopped and began to tread water as he stared in amazement. That stone wall directly ahead of him seemed to remain intact and unbroken, yet the boat had suddenly vanished right through it. It was as though the wall had reached out and swallowed up both boat and oarsman.

CHAPTER 11
TRAIL OF THE CRIME BEAST

CARSON WAS suddenly aware of a strange, low rumble coming to his ears across the water from the direction of the stone end of the wharf. Would that have anything to do with the vanishing of the boat? Of course, it was dark and he could only see shadowy forms dimly; otherwise, he realized, he might be able to tell what had happened to the craft.

The young explorer began swimming toward that black wall through which the boat had slipped. Funny about that! The boat and the oarsman had just seemed to melt into the barricade. He thought of several solutions, all of them wildly fantastic. Perhaps that boat had gone down a chute under the stones. But that was ridiculous, for there was no division to keep the water out of any depression or slide that might be there.

Rod Carson stared at the lower part of the wall. Was it moving or was it merely his imagination? He thought the bottom of the wall was tipping out at him as though a trap door were closing.

Something else arose to make Carson's situation more perilous than ever. He heard a gentle swishing sound not ten feet from him, followed by a splash. He felt something rub over his back and vanish. In sudden panic he turned his head and as he did so, he saw a small object in the water not far from him. It looked as though the point of a great knife were sticking above the surface, but he knew that wasn't the case. The water was infested with man-eating sharks.

Now Carson was swimming like mad for the stone wall. He was a powerful swimmer and as he went, he splashed with all his might, floundering about in an effort to drive the sharks off. He had heard that they were harmless if scared by splashing water, but he had never tested them himself.

Something brushed the top of Carson's legs and there was a splash behind him. He whirled his head, saw another dorsal fin behind him. He kicked out and splashed harder than ever.

He was almost at the stone wall. But what would he do when

he reached it? That wall looked perfectly blank now, with no visible entry. If there was a trick way of getting in, he wouldn't know it. Then suddenly, he struck something under the water right in front of him.

It was like a long arm, reaching ten or twelve feet out from that stone wall. It was only three or four inches under water but it wasn't floating. He felt it give a little under his weight as he came upon it. The fins of those sharks were coming closer. Carson splashed again, kicked and flailed his arms around. What was this arm or beam that stuck out in the water? Would that lead to anything?

To Carson's ears came that rumbling sound again. Something was happening, moving before him. As though the stones in the wall ahead were like a cleverly devised folding door, a space just large enough to admit a man and a rowboat opened up to admit Carson. The jam that he had struck with his fist sank away with a sudden burst of speed and Rod Carson darted ahead into the opening. His out flung hands touched the row boat just inside and again there was another jam like a two by four extending just out of the water inside.

Carson clutched the end of a small row-boat, pulled himself over the side, and let the water trail from his clothes. He untied the bundle that he had made out of his coat and made a hasty investigation. Yes, the flash light was all right. He put his hand in front of the lens and pressed the button. That worked O.K. His gun was in working order, too, he noted thankfully.

The young explorer walked carefully in the front of the boat, feeling his way, and climbed onto the dock itself. His ears strained to catch some sound that would tell him where the agent of Wu Fang had gone, but the only noise that came to him was the thumping of his heart.

For several minutes, he groped his way trying not to make any more noise than necessary, as he searched for an entrance opening. His efforts were in vain. Panic was beginning to seize him for he knew that Wu Fang's agent was getting farther away all the time.

He was too late he told himself. Everything had been closed up behind this agent of the yellow fiend. There was some trick passage, some trick opening that a secret button would move but now there was no chance of finding it.

Carson was about to turn back when suddenly his foot struck something. It was the edge of a raised board in the floor.

Instantly he knelt down and began tugging at it. His heart leaped and began pounding wildly when he found that it moved. He struggled to get it up and it came grudgingly. His light beam slithered down into the opening and he saw steps leading off toward land.

Quickly, Carson slipped down the steps, so overjoyed at finding this passage that he paid little attention to the fact that his light was on. He was running now, gun in one band and light in the other. The walls of the stone passage were wet and damp and glistening in the reflection of the light beam.

Down ahead, Carson could make out what appeared to be the end of the corridor. If this was a blind alley, then somewhere along that corridor was a secret door that led into another passage. But on reaching the end, he found that he was going up a slight incline.

A QUEER little chill ran up Carson's back as he realized that the beam of his flashlight was becoming a sickly yellow, and that his battery was giving out. He snapped off his electric torch to save it and moved on, groping his way. It was horribly dark in there with the light off. Well, he could only follow the passage and do his best. At any rate, he had his gun held ready; he didn't expect that to go back on him.

Carson tried to figure out where he was going underground. After leaving the dock, the ceiling of the passage had risen to

a little better than six feet. That permitted him to see easily, standing erect. That also meant that the passage had risen to higher ground away from the wharf. He remembered also that the Chinese quarter in Singapore was on a rise of ground above the level of the harbor. According to that, then, he was going into the very bowels of Singapore's Chinatown.

Slowly, a strange feeling was gripping Carson, a feeling that he was being watched and followed. He took extreme precaution to move on tip toe and to make his way slowly.

The water was infested with man-eating sharks.

Carson waited tensely with his automatic cocked, but minutes passed and he couldn't hear a sound. In disgust, he arose.

He had lost the trail of Wu Fang's agent and he couldn't pick it up again. Still, he asked himself, what was he kicking about? He had followed the passage through without branching out in any direction. Certainly, he couldn't go wrong on that.

Suddenly, he came up against a dead end. He groped about, feeling the walls, then sensed a draft of air blowing on his forehead. That must come from above and yet—

In desperation, he snapped the button of his flashlight, but it was no use, for the generators were dead.

He had just turned and was going back to the dead end of the passage, when suddenly he heard a voice in the darkness. It came in a low whisper and it spoke his name.

"Rod Carson."

Instantly, Carson whirled around and his gun hand slashed through space.

Not another sound came as he groped about. He could feel nothing but the walls about him.

"Rod Carson."

The voice came again. This time Carson stopped, and listened as his name was repeated.

Suddenly, he remembered the draft that was hitting him on the forehead. That was it. There was an open space up there. He flung his left hand toward the ceiling and groped about frantically as his name was spoken again in a sweet, innocent voice.

"Rod Carson, up here," it said.

The voice was barely audible, yet Carson could feel a definite presence near him. A faint, lovely perfume mingled strangely with the dank, musty smell of the stone passage.

Rod Carson would recognize that presence anywhere.

"Tanya," he called softly. "Tanya, what are you doing here? Help me."

"Sssh! Someone may hear you. Here, feel about," came the voice.

Something whizzed through the air past Carson's face. He caught hold of it, found that it was a rope about an inch and a half in diameter. "Climb up," Tanya breathed.

In three quick hand over hand strokes, Rod Carson gripped the edge of the dead end wall and pulled himself up. He felt Tanya's hand beneath his one arm, helping him. Then he and the girl were facing each other in the pitch darkness. He felt Tanya's warm breath on his cheek.

"You should not have come," she said. "Didn't you get my note?"

"Yes," Carson said. "Thank heaven we did get it. That's why we got the electricity turned off in Singapore.

"It was done just in time," Tanya said. "But I'm afraid—"

"Afraid of what?" Carson said, placing his hand on the girl's trembling shoulder.

"Afraid for you," she whispered softly.

"Don't worry about me," Carson said reassuringly. "I'll be O.K. Who sent you here, Tanya?"

Carson felt the girl stiffen suddenly.

"Do I have to be sent everywhere that I go?" she asked.

"I had hoped not," Carson said. "Where's Wu Fang?"

"I do not think I should tell you," the girl said. "I am sure you could do nothing to stop him."

Carson emitted a hoarse, low chuckle, utterly devoid of humor.

"Well, you've got to admit that we have done pretty well so far," he said, "by getting the lights turned off and keeping that yellow devil guessing about—"

"Yes," Tanya interrupted. "I thought that was it. You are keeping him guessing about the trip that you and Mr. Kildare made to the home of Mr. Archibald Cameron. That was a trick, wasn't it?"

Carson stiffened suddenly, and with his left hand he sprang forward and gripped the girl by the shoulder.

"Listen," Carson growled. "Is that why you are here? Did you come here to get that information for Wu Fang?"

"No, no," Tanya breathed. "Please, Rod. You hurt me. I didn't come here for that purpose. I swear it."

Instantly, Carson was filled with remorse.

"I am sorry," he said, "but you know what it does to me, Tanya, to see you in the power of that yellow devil. You're far too lovely, too beautiful, to be dominated by a beast like that."

Tanya was straightening again, growing stiff and rigid and cold. Carson felt her hands on his wrists, let his arms drop from her shoulder. Then he was surprised to feel her cold, firm hand in his. It was not an affectionate gesture and he recognized it at once as an act of guidance.

At the same time, Tanya said in a low voice, vibrant with

emotion, "Come. I will prove to you whether I am here to get information from you."

Carson didn't know how the girl could move so skillfully in this dark place without a light of any kind. She must have made this trip many times, must know every step from memory.

Then suddenly, her hand stopped him. "We are here now," she whispered. "Only one set of doors, one partition separates you from Wu Fang."

And now Carson was aware of the fact that there was a very dim light illuminating the place from somewhere. He reached for his gun but froze suddenly, as he discovered the pocket where he had dropped his gun was empty.

CHAPTER 12
WU FANG APPEARS

CARSON'S TEMPER suddenly got the better of him. He whirled around and grasped Tanya by the arm, pressing his fingers in her flesh until she winced.

"You treacherous she-devil!" he rasped, "You took my gun. You've led me into a trap."

Carson felt the girl shudder under the pressure of his fingers.

"Rod, please!" she choked. "You're hurting me. Your gun is gone? When did you miss it?"

"You know," Carson rasped. "You know all about it. I've got a good mind to—"

Suddenly Tanya was shaking convulsively, and he heard a sound come from her that he couldn't quite understand. Tanya was weeping softly. Instantly, Carson snapped out of his anger and let go of the girl's arm.

"Sorry," he snapped. "I didn't know I was playing with an infant when I grabbed you like that."

Tanya was still weeping softly.

"It—isn't that," she choked. "You could go on hurting me forever—physically—and I wouldn't mind if only you would trust me. There won't be much time. I feel it coming. I won't be trustworthy much longer. But I was, I was! Your gun is gone and that means—"

Suddenly the girl was straightening with a great effort.

"Yes," Carson went on brutally, "my gun is gone and that means you took it."

"No, no," Tanya sobbed. "Oh, what's the use? How can I tell you? How can I explain? We're in this together now and I—I'll suffer more than you will. I feel I'm changing already. I'm losing my grip on myself."

Carson touched her arm.

"What do you mean, Tanya?" he asked. "I'll trust you. But what do you mean by saying Wu Fang is taking command of you?"

"You don't understand," the girl sobbed, "and I can't explain it. I felt free a little while ago. That is why I was able to come to you and try to lead you to Wu Fang. I have led you this far and"—she stiffened with an effort—"I will lead you the rest of the way now in spite of—"

Tanya broke off in a spasm of sobs.

"But, please, please, Rod," she said, "don't think I took your gun. I didn't."

At that moment the seriousness of the situation dawned on Carson.

"Good Heavens!" he hissed. "You mean then that someone removed the gun from my pocket while we were moving along the passage? They know then that you are leading me to Wu Fang?"

"Yes," the girl said.

"I can't let you go through with this," Carson said. "I'm going to get you out of here and get you clear before Wu Fang can do anything to you."

"Yes," Tanya admitted, "but don't worry about me. Get Wu Fang. Stop him from—"

Carson suddenly put his arm around Tanya and drew her back the way they had come.

"We're going out," he said decisively.

Then suddenly he slammed up against something, a heavy panel that blocked his way. Frantically he moved to the side, still trying to find an exit. He swung around and faced the girl.

"Tanya," he said, "do you know what room this is?"

"Yes," she said, "its Wu Fang's paneled room. All newcomers are confined here until the Master looks them over. Then—"

"And all these panels raise then?" Carson asked quickly.

"Yes," Tanya said, "they all operate by buttons."

"Do you know how to get through any of them?" Carson demanded.

"I believe I know how to get through one if the safety hasn't been set on the other side," Tanya said.

She leaped away and Carson followed her.

"There," she said, reaching a slight depression in the heavy framework. "I press this part and the machinery is set in operation so that the panel raises."

Carson felt Tanya pressing the bit of wood, felt her fall back.

She spun around and faced him, then flew to him like a frightened child. Another sound had come to them, a high-pitched whine, scarcely audible.

"The panels are opening!" she gasped. "Not the one that I started but others. We're—we're—"

Her voice broke off abruptly and as though by a great force, she was brutally drawn away from Carson. The young explorer felt himself hurled back; the attack was so sudden that it caught him off guard. Tanya was away from him now.

As Carson shifted to the side, arms were thrown about his neck and head, twisting them cruelly. He side-stepped and crouched, bringing the smelly figure whose arms were about his neck well over on his back.

He heard a grunt as he hurled his adversary crashing to the floor.

Now Rod Carson struck out savagely with both fists.

Wham!

Bam!

He couldn't see distinctly what he was doing. Powerful arms seized him about the waist. He fought vainly to shake that assailant off as he caught a blow in the face.

Suddenly, both his arms were seized from behind and bent upward from between his shoulder blades. He winced with pain but managed to keep from crying out.

He was bent double, now, and couldn't move to shake himself free. There were more of those smelly rat men about him, holding him and the human beast who had his arms doubled up behind him lessened the pressure a little to let him stand alone.

Again came that high-pitched whining sound. Carson knew now that it was the sound of the lifting device opening another panel. A light shone in, and into it stepped a familiar figure. It was Wu Fang, the Dragon Lord of Crime—Wu Fang, with his yellow silk robe embroidered across the front with a dragon. Wu Fang of the long, thin face with the pinched chin and the cruel, thin lips and the wide forehead.

The yellow demon was smiling as his eyes shifted from Tanya to Carson, then back to Tanya.

"I was afraid of this, my lovely one," he said, addressing the girl. "I was afraid that when I put you to the test you would fail me. But you are my favorite, my beautiful one, and so I will be kind to you."

The Dragon Lord of Crime turned to Carson.

"You have made great explorations," he said, "but I have something, I believe, which you have never seen. I have had it built since I heard about the hanging gardens in Babylon and the activity there. But my hanging gardens"—here Wu Fang's smile broadened—"are quite different from the hanging gardens of Babylon. However, they are built for the purpose of hanging, and I shall let you have a glimpse of them, Mr. Carson."

125

The green eyes of Wu Fang glowed fiendishly.

"You see," he said, "they are just taking down the body of one of your predecessors, Mr. Carson."

The young explorer was suddenly transfixed with horror at what he saw. Wu Fang's hanging garden was a riot of luxurious, concentrated profusion of oriental plants of every description. The space was too small to permit the growth of trees, but rare shrubs, large and small, were substituted.

IN THE center of this garden was a slightly-raised platform from where three vile agents of Wu Fang were carrying the body of a man from a hole in the platform. There was a rope around his neck, a rope now limp.

A flat-faced, flat-nosed, bull-necked squat beast of a man jabbered and cackled to a dozen-odd hideous beasts that scampered about the platform and the floor. Could this be the keeper of the death beasts, the one that had been called Djiga?

But Carson got only a glimpse of the beasts and their keeper, as his main attention was focused on the body that was being carried away. It was dressed in a tweed suit that he recognized as Kildare's.

One of the agents lifted the noose from the limp neck and let the head flop back.

"The hanging gardens," Wu Fang chuckled, "they are a very nice idea, are they not? You see, Mr. Carson, I have changed. Instead of making death a hideous performance, I have suddenly become aware of the fact that it can be made beautiful. You could not choose a more beautiful spot in which to die than in a beautiful garden like this, could you?"

Now Carson's anger, which had been rising all the time to a feverish pitch suddenly burst forth.

"You yellow rat!" he cracked. "You've got the upper hand now but you won't go on forever. We've stopped you in this electricity menace. You won't admit it but your back is to the wall. You are not going to gain anything by killing Tanya, if that's your idea."

"Oh, but you are wrong, Mr. Carson," Wu Fang said suavely. "You see, I will gain something. Tanya had her chance, but she has failed, and now my punishment of her will serve to put her out of the way so that I will never need to distrust her any more. It will also serve as an example to others who might be tempted to destroy me."

Wu Fang turned toward the limp body that was being carried out. He nodded and smiled at Carson.

"You see," he went on, "how foolish it is for you to speak in that way, for already they are carrying out the body of my greatest enemy, Mr. Kildare."

"You're a li—"

Carson tried to choke off that last word but it was too late. Wu Fang knew what was up. He nodded, and a cruel smile crossed his lips.

"I see," he said, "you know, too, that this gentleman has been substituted for Mr. Kildare. Yes, it grieves me to have to hang Sir Reginald Owen. I might have done much with that honorable gentleman had he wished to work with me. But now"— the sloping shoulders of the yellow fiend shrugged—"it is too late, and it is time for Tanya to receive her punishment."

Tanya's expression when Wu Fang looked at her was one of horror and fear, but slowly it changed to a look of peace. The brown-skinned, half-naked beasts that held Tanya seemed to understand, as they unclenched their dark, filthy fingers from her graceful white arms.

The girl stood alone, unhampered and free physically, but Carson saw that she was held by a much stronger power than any physical bindings could exert. She was under the spell of Wu Fang.

Carson suddenly went half mad as he saw the yellow beast start toward her. He jerked his right arm free from the beasts who were holding him and lashed out fiercely.

But there was a savage onrush as three dark bodies came hurling at him, bearing him down, and twisting his arms behind his back again.

Meanwhile Wu Fang hadn't made a move. He had simply stood away from the door, while Tanya, as though walking in her sleep, had been approaching him gracefully and delicately—like a rabbit drawn irresistibly to a snake.

Carson was bent over with pain as his arms were forced back. Now his captors permitted him to straighten, and he could see Tanya again. She had reached Wu Fang and was passing him. The yellow beast shot a triumphant glance at Carson.

"You see," he smiled hideously, "they all obey my commands. And you—very soon now you will be walking in there. Within a few minutes, the punishment of Tanya will be completed and I will come then for you."

Carson felt a twinge of pain as his arms were trussed up

again. Ropes were being fastened about his wrists and feet, and he heard the clanking of the ring in the floor that Wu Fang had mentioned.

His captors left him there on the floor with his face turned toward the hanging gardens entrance, which was covered over, in part, with vines. A strange light was burning down into this pit. It appeared to be some strange electrical device to take the place of the sun, and furnish light for the growth of these flowers and plants. But how could that be? All the electrical power in Singapore was turned off.

Carson suddenly ceased pondering on that, for he could see Tanya still moving very slowly toward the little platform.

The young explorer's mind was a wild tangle of incoherent thoughts. Djiga was there waiting beside the scaffold with his devilish rat beasts perched on his head, shoulders, and arms. Beasts that stroked his stinking flesh and waited for the command to strike out and kill. But why were the beasts there when Tanya was to be hung?

With bulging eyes he watched Tanya as she lifted her long dress daintily with one hand and placed her foot on the platform. Wu Fang was suddenly beside her to gallantly assist her onto the platform where a yellow beast was holding the noose to place around her neck.

Carson suddenly burst forth in a powerful effort to free himself. As he struggled, he cried out at the top of his voice, "Tanya, Tanya, don't you know what you're doing? Don't you realize that you're going to be killed? Don't let them—"

CHAPTER 13
THE TRAP OF WU FANG

IN SPITE of his half-insane rage, Carson realized that his yelling was doing no good, since Tanya was completely held in Wu Fang's power. Both her shapely little feet were on the platform a foot or so above the floor. Without a word from anyone, she stopped, while Djiga bent forward, the savage beasts still clinging to his head and arms as he fixed the trap door for Tanya to stand on. He brought it up and fastened it, latching it from below, so that when the signal was given, the door would give way and Tanya's body would shoot down the few remaining inches to the floor and be suspended there.

Djiga stepped back to the side of the platform and placed his hand on a lever extending from it. Now Tanya stepped forward until she was standing directly on the trap door. An almost black Malayan came forward with a rope.

Carson writhed and fought more savagely, as from somewhere above, the rope was made taut.

All was ready now. Nothing could save Tanya. Wu Fang spoke to one of his Chinese servants in Cantonese. The servant stepped forward and bound the girl's hands behind her.

Suddenly, Wu Fang raised his long-nailed fingers before the girl and his eyes glowed green again as he said, "I give you up, Tanya."

Instantly, the girl's expression changed; her mouth dropped open and she started about with a horrified expression.

"Wu Fang!" she cried. "Master! What are you going to do with me? Where is Rod Carson? What have you—"

"Mr. Rod Carson is still alive," Wu Fang smiled calmly. "He will be punished next. I bring you back to your own senses so that you may realize what I am doing to you. But as you have been my favorite one, the torture will not be for long."

Wu Fang continued to talk in the same hideous tone, but Carson was paying no attention to him now. Something was taking place behind him.

A voice out of the darkness that he recognized as Kildare's said "Hold still. Don't move. Don't cry out. I'm here."

Then Carson felt the ropes about his wrists loosen, felt the vibration of a sharp blade being drawn over them. He turned his head and saw Kildare crouching there.

"Tanya!" Carson gasped under his breath. "She's in there. They're going to hang her. They got Sir Reginald."

"Jove," Kildare exclaimed. "What a pity."

Another slash and Carson's legs were freed. "Come on," he hissed, and with Kildare following, he charged headlong to the underground hanging garden of Wu Fang.

All was set for the kill. Wu Fang had stepped back, had raised his hand to give the signal. Djiga, keeper of the death beasts, had his hand on the lever that would spring the trap door.

As Carson charged in, Kildare yelled, "Grab Tanya! Hold her up. I'll cut her loose!"

At their entrance, the poison lizard beasts, frogs, and the tiny deadly snakes slithered off Djiga's arms, shoulders, and head and dropped on the platform, apparently in sudden fright. There was a wild cry of rage from Wu Fang as he leaped back. Carson sprang to the platform and as he lunged through the air, he lashed out with his right hand, caught Djiga squarely on his flat nose and hurled him back.

Carson put his arm around Tanya's waist and caught her up. As Kildare leaped, there was the glitter of a knife flashing through the air.

Carson was struggling wildly to keep his balance, but he went down and Tanya with him. There was another cry of rage from Wu Fang that turned suddenly into a cry of pain.

Total darkness suddenly took possession of the place. Then, as Carson struggled erect with Tanya in his arms, there was a flash. Kildare's automatic blasted out. A cry of pain answered the shot, and again the automatic blasted.

There was a grinding sound, a shrill whine and a boom, as though a heavy door had closed. Then suddenly there was nothing but silence.

"Carson is that you?" asked the voice of Val Kildare. "Quick!" he continued. "We're shut in here. I'll strike a match. Do you know anyway to get out of this place?"

A match flared, lighting the interior of the garden dimly. The shadows of the trees and shrubbery danced grotesquely. Carson stared about in the weird light.

"They've all gone," he said in bewilderment.

"Yes," Kildare said. "Fighting in the dark was too much for all of them. We've got to be leaving too or—"

"Yes, yes," Tanya choked. "I know. Listen. This can be made into a death chamber very quickly. You perhaps thought Wu

Fang was going to let you live after he left us. But he has gone for a reason."

"A death chamber," Kildare repeated. "You mean gas?"

Tanya had wriggled a little out of Carson's arms so that she stood up but she still clung to him.

"Yes," she said, "I think its gas. I know he had this room built so that he could escape from attackers, trap them in here, and kill them."

"But there must be some way out," Kildare said. "Don't you know where it is?"

The girl was shaking; Carson drew her closer to him.

"Yes," she whispered. "There is a way. Let me think. If I could only—"

Kildare lighted another match while Carson became aware of a strange odor filtering into the underground garden.

"The gas!" he cried in alarm.

"Yes," Kildare said. "I smell it."

Bam!

There came the sound of sudden stamping as a light flared in Kildare's hand.

"Get Tanya off the floor," he cried. "Those beasts are coming back."

In panic, Carson grasped Tanya to protect her. He felt something leap upon her, and struck savagely at the thing. Again and again he beat at it.

"Rod, Rod!" Tanya was screaming. "It's on me! It's—"

Wham!

With all his might, the young explorer struck at the thing, hurled it with a crash against the wall.

"Think, Tanya!" Carson cried. "How do we get out of here? Quick! The beasts are all over the place!"

KILDARE'S MATCH went out and when he lighted another one, Carson saw that he had torn up one of the shrubs by the roots and was beating the floor and the air with it as tiny beasts, rat-headed lizards and horny toads and snakes came leaping at him from the floor and from above.

Tanya was crying, "Wait! Wait! I think I have it! Over there! Quick! Press that piece of wood that sticks out from the wall."

In a fleet second, they were at the indicated spot.

"There," Tanya said, "that's it." She reached up and touched it herself. "It doesn't work!" she cried. "The electricity is turned off or something. But I think the door is unlocked."

Something came flying through the air at Carson's head just as the match that Kildare was holding went out.

"Tanya!" Kildare cried. "Can you stand alone?"

"Yes," the girl said. "I want to help. What can I do?"

Kildare didn't have time to stop and explain. He had a club in his hands now and he was flailing the floor of the garden.

"In my right hand coat pocket there's a box of matches," he cried. "Get them out and light them. Carson get a club. We've got to kill these beasts before—"

The government man broke off in a series of coughs.

"That gas will get us if the beasts don't," he spluttered.

Tanya sprang to his side. Carson fumbled about for a club, pulled up shrubbery and plants and small trees out of the garden.

The fight went on with Tanya lighting matches. All three of them were coughing now. Things were getting hazy before Carson's eyes as the gas slowly but surely took effect.

"Tanya, which panel is it that opens?" Carson cried.

"The one that you came through over there," the girl answered, pointing. "Try it."

Kildare suddenly leaped beside Carson, while Tanya cried, "I'll try to take care of the beasts. You raise the door if you can."

Both men were seized by another fit of coughing. The door gave grudgingly inch by inch, but they were forcing it past something that held it all but locked. Four inches, five inches, six inches, eight inches of space beneath it.

Wham!

Bam!

Tanya was beating a rapid tattoo on the floor with her club. Then suddenly, she was beside them, coughing.

"Let me help," she gasped. "I think the animals are—"

Again she coughed. Placing herself between Carson and Kildare, she strained and pulled with all her might on the door. It rose a little faster now. There was a space of a foot under it.

"Tanya," Carson said, "you slide under."

"Not until you do," she cried.

"All right, maybe that would be better."

Carson dropped to the floor. He was so dizzy that he wondered if he would be able to get up again. He wriggled like a snake under the door.

"Come on, Tanya," he said. "You can make it."

The girl was crawling after him while Carson struggled to his hands and knees.

"I'll hold it up, Kildare, while you come," he called.

Then the government man was sliding beneath the panel. The great door boomed as it fell again.

"God," Kildare exclaimed. Do you smell the gas?"

Carson sniffed. "Yes," he said.

"Stay close to the floor," Kildare advised. "The air is purer down there. We learned that in the lower chamber of the hanging gardens. Keep Tanya down there, too."

"But can't we lift one of the doors like we did the other one?" Carson gasped.

"No," Kildare said. "I tried that. There isn't a bit of give to any of them. We've first got to release the secret lock or we'll be gassed in here like three rats."

CHAPTER 14
CHAMBER OF TORTURE

CARSON WAS on the floor near Tanya. Desperately, he spoke to the beautiful girl.

"Are you all right?" he asked.

Tanya's eyes shifted to him and then away.

"I'm getting dizzy," she said.

Carson rubbed his hand over her forehead very lightly and patted her shoulder.

"Tanya," he said. "Tanya, listen. You've got to try to remember where the secret release is that will let us out of this place. Can't you think of some buttons or levers or something?"

Carson saw the girl's eyes flicker a little with sudden dizziness. Then they closed as consciousness left her.

"Kildare," Carson choked, "we've got to find a way out ourselves. Tanya has fainted."

Kildare didn't answer. Carson whirled around, rolling over on the floor. The room spun about him.

Thud!

That sound gave Carson a sudden start and he realized that something was pawing at his foot and leg. He jerked it away. Then there was a fit of insistent coughing near by.

"It's me," Kildare gasped. "About done for. Trying to find a secret button or lever. You dizzy, too, Rod?"

"Yes," Carson said. "Got to get out."

There came a low, rumbling sound that lasted only a short moment. Carson tried to turn his head, to roll his eyes, but he didn't even have the strength to do that. He did, however, manage to see a form creeping toward them.

At first, it looked like a huge alligator crawling across the floor, dragging its belly. He could make out something that looked like a great snout. Was this all his imagination or was it really true? Carson couldn't tell for certain.

The beastly thing had stopped near Kildare for a moment, but now it was sliding on toward Carson. The young explorer felt a hand on his foot. It moved up his ankle, then up his leg, raising his trousers with the movement. Carson felt the distinct prick of a needle in the flesh of his leg. He was aware of a sudden numbing sensation enveloping him.

A strange paralysis had gripped him, but still he managed to roll his head slightly to follow the movements of the beast-like thing. It was moving toward Tanya now.

The nerves of Carson's eyes seemed to be functioning all right, but that was all the control he had over his body. He saw the beast drag across the floor and reach out. No, that wasn't a beast; that was a man paralyzed from the hips down. He could drag himself by the arms but that was all. No, Carson was wrong in that guess for those legs moved a little to one side and then to the other. But what was that ugly, blunt snout on the man if he was human?

Then suddenly Carson divined the answer. The man was wearing a gas mask and that, in all probability, was the reason why he clung to the floor to be down where the air would be a little less dangerous.

One clawed hand was groping along the floor almost blindly in the direction of Tanya's ankles. As she had fallen there on the floor, the silken folds of her dress had caught part way up to her knee. The clutching hand of that crawling man-beast was groping up her leg. The movement was almost a caress.

It drove Carson almost mad to be compelled to lie there and watch that ugly crawler. He saw his hand come down, saw that he was drawing down the girl's stocking. That was it. He was making her leg bare for the injection of the paralyzing fluid.

As Carson lay there, he could see very dimly the fingers of the beast-man toying with the little hypodermic device. He imagined he could see the grin on the crawler's face as he slowly pressed the needle beneath the white flesh of Tanya's neck. The girl didn't move an inch while the plunger was being thrust in.

Then the crawler turned and surveyed Carson and Kildare through the great staring eyes of the gas mask. He stared back once more at Tanya, then slithered around, vanished into the darkness.

It seemed to Rod Carson that they lay there for hours. By now his mind was growing perfectly clear, but his body was hopelessly paralyzed. He could roll his eyeballs and stare about. His eyes seemed to be the only things he could control.

Carson thought he heard that rumbling sound again. No, this was a higher-pitched noise. There were voices, one in particular that he recognized, and out of the blackness on his left came a figure, a tall; narrow-shouldered man dressed in a yellow silken robe with a queer Chinese tasseled cap on his head. The long face was grinning, and the slant eyes were radiant with a hideous green light.

Wu Fang stood triumphantly before them and with his coming the paneled room was suddenly filled with a weird light.

"I see that you have not left as yet," he laughed fiendishly. "That is well, for I have something I think you will enjoy watching before you escape."

What did Wu Fang mean? Did he really mean that they were going to escape? Carson's heart leaped, but his hopes fell when he saw what came next Agents of Wu Fang were bringing in a man. Like themselves, he appeared to be paralyzed, although his eyes were open, and he could stare about.

In the strange light that permeated the room, Carson recognized him. It was Archibald Cameron, the head of the power and light company that furnished electricity to Singapore.

Cameron stared down at Kildare, Carson, and Tanya lying on the floor with great fear in his eyes. Other agents followed behind those who were carrying the power magnate.

THE STUB of rope that hung from above could still be seen through the door. But that apparently wasn't playing any part in the horrible ceremony that was to come. Wu Fang spoke again in his mixture of Malayan and Cantonese and immediately, the three giant Chinese brutes carrying Cameron, set him on his feet. Two of them held him while the third vanished from view, only to return presently with a heavy timber in his hand.

"Now you are mine, Tanya," the beast man gloated.

There were notches in the floor and ceiling into which the timber fitted. Moreover, now that the timber was in place in a vertical position over the center of the garden, a brace of solid wood extended horizontally from the heavier timber about four feet up from the floor.

They moved Cameron to this timber and held him so that he stood with his face and chest and stomach against it. Two of the agents extended his arms, one on either side of the timber and along the outstretched beam that reached almost to the end of his finger tips. A rope was produced and Cameron's body was quickly bound to the pillar. After the body was fastened, the rope was wound around his arms so that when the tying was done, Cameron appeared to be stiffly embracing this vertical timber except that his arms extended straight out in front of him and were fastened to the horizontal beam, while the hands were stretched out, palms down.

Wu Fang gave an order in English and another servant appeared. A half-caste from Indo-China, Carson guessed. His head sloped sharply back as though there were no space left for his brain and his lips were so thin that they failed to cover his mouthful of teeth. His eyes above his hawk-like nose were wild and staring like the eyes of a lunatic, and more than that, they were crossed.

"Zaru," Wu Fang said, "I desire that the gentleman has his full senses of feeling returned to him. You will see to it with the needle?"

The cross-eyed half-human bowed without a single change of expression on his hideous face.

"Yes, Master," he said.

Then suddenly, Zaru stopped in the doorway and those wide, staring eyes took in Kildare, Carson, and Tanya who were lying on the floor. As his gaze rested on Tanya, a look of repulsive greed and lust came into Zaru's eyes.

Wu Fang's voice came again, "Zaru, I have ordered."

Zaru turned with a jerky motion and bowed. From the pocket of his filthy robe, he took a hypodermic needle. He faced Archibald Cameron and his long arm and ham-like hand flashed out to the man's collar. Then with a blunt thump, he pushed the plunger down.

There was almost instant reaction from Cameron, who began to struggle frantically.

"I tell you I know nothing about it," he cried out. "I have told you all I know. What are you going to do with me?"

Cameron's eyes were bulging in awful fear of what was to come. "I have asked for the truth," Wu Fang said. "I will have the truth, Mr. Cameron."

"I'll tell you the truth," Cameron said. "Anything that you want to know. But for the sake of humanity, don't torture me. Don't go on with this awful thing that you plan."

Wu Fang stepped a little closer, and now from one of the folds of his robe, Carson saw that he had produced a pair of pliers. Their jaws were queer-shaped, partly round. In the next instant, Carson realized what was taking place. Wu Fang was going to pluck the man's fingernails out until he got the information he sought.

Even now as he watched the yellow beast was holding one of Cameron's fingers, and fastening the pliers ends to the nail.

Cameron was crying out, "No, no, not that! I tell you I have told you the truth. I—"

Wu Fang's hand clenched the pliers. He didn't jerk hard and quickly; instead, he pulled slowly, deliberately harder and harder. Cameron's mouth opened wide, his eyes rolled, and he screamed with awful fear and pain. Again and again he shrieked as Wu Fang continued to pull. Then the Dragon Lord of Crime held the nail in the tweezers, while the end of the finger was a mass of blood and raw flesh. He dropped the gruesome object to the floor and opened the pliers again.

Now Mr. Cameron," he said as he held the pliers poised in the air, "I have given you a demonstration of the beginning of the torture. If you do not tell me the truth, there are nine other fingers from which the nails can be pulled in the same manner."

"I'll tell you!" Cameron gasped. "Anything you want to know. But for God's sake, don't do that again. Spare me!"

"I want to know," Wu Fang said calmly, "the truth about the visit that Mr. Carson and Mr. Kildare made to your house earlier in the evening. You and your engineers are supposed to know of a counteracting current that will act in reverse and kill me and my men if we try to use our generators in the Singapore circuit to cause mass death."

"I have already told you," Cameron choked.

Mentally, Carson stiffened. His ears were tingling to catch the next words.

"I have already told you," Cameron said, "that it was all a

joke. Just a story made up so that you would send your agents to listen and we could find out where you were hiding. It was all the idea of Kildare and Carson. Kildare was trailing your men."

Wu Fang nodded.

"Yes," he said. "I know that. But that is not the truth."

Suddenly, the yellow fiend flew into a rage. He snatched the next fingernail between the jaws of the tweezers, pulled slowly, firmly. Again he seized the next one, pulled both of them and dropped them to the floor while Cameron screamed in horrible agony.

"It's the truth!" he yelled desperately. "I can not tell you any more. That's all I know."

"You lie!" Wu Fang said and again he proceeded to pull the nails. He had finished with the one hand and was going on the other when Cameron fainted. The Dragon Lord of Crime stood up and straightened.

"Djiga," he said in a low voice.

The flat-nosed, flat-faced keeper of the beasts stepped into Carson's line of vision.

"Cameron has told the truth," Wu Fang said. "It was a trick by Kildare. I am safe now in going to the power house. Everything will be arranged."

He nodded at a red and green striped reptile about a foot long that Djiga held to his cheek while the snake caressed his neck.

"Let that be the end of Mr. Cameron," Wu Fang pronounced softly.

Djiga nodded, stepped beside Cameron, held the snake out and muttered a few unintelligible words. Quicker than the eye could follow, the poison viper lashed out, sank its fangs into the neck of Archibald Cameron, clung there a moment while it forced the deadly poison from its fangs into the body. Then it drew out the fangs and coiled affectionately about the keeper's hand. Djiga retreated out of sight.

WU FANG spoke in a mixture of Chinese and Malayan again. The agents left Archibald Cameron's body lashed to the post and filed out into the panel room once more. After the others had passed through, Wu Fang reached his long right arm up to the ceiling and slid back a panel revealing an electric light socket. He produced a bulb from under his robe and screwed it in. Up to now, he hadn't uttered a word to his captors who were still paralyzed on the floor, but now he turned and addressed them.

"At last," he said, "Wu Fang is victorious. My men are waiting at the power house for me where the electricity will soon be turned on. We have our death generators attached to the line. Less than an hour from now, more than a million people in Singapore will die."

Carson shifted his eyes to Tanya, realizing that she must be conscious now. She was staring with frightened eyes at her master.

"You will all die," Wu Fang said, "by this electric bulb."

Carson was thinking frantically of one angle. This thing wouldn't work. Kildare had gotten the order from the governor general to turn off the electricity, but now the government man was here, paralyzed. Wu Fang was staring down at Carson now, smiling and chuckling to himself.

"I quite read your mind, Mr. Carson," he said. "You are correct. Without Mr. Kildare to intercede with the governor general so that the lights would be turned back on, I would be powerless, so"—the yellow devil turned—"I have arranged a substitute. Permit me to introduce Mr. Val Kildare in person."

Wu Fang turned toward the panel that led out of the passage. His green eyes glowed and he gave a short nod. A man stepped into the room. To Rod Carson's astonishment, he saw that the fellow was the image of Kildare. He was the same height, had the same features and hair, and wore the same tweed suit. But the voice, how would that fit in?

Wu Fang turned and addressed the newcomer.

"You are ready to aid me, Mr. Kildare?" he asked. The man nodded.

"Yes," he said, "quite ready, Wu Fang. I shall go to the home of the governor general and assure him that everything is under perfect control. I'll tell him you have been captured and that it is quite safe to permit the lights to be turned on in Singapore once more."

"Excellent," Wu Fang nodded. "You will go at once. And I—I will go to the power house with my men and see that there is no halt in our plans."

The tall man turned and went out again into the passage. Wu Fang smiled.

"I doubt if Mr. Kildare himself would be able to tell the

difference," he said. "The likeness is striking, is it not, Mr. Kildare?"

Now Rod Carson's eyes shifted to the figure below. He couldn't feel Kildare's head on his leg any longer, but as he strained to see in that direction, he saw Kildare lying there. The paralysis in Carson's leg prevented him from feeling the weight of the government man's body.

Still chuckling to himself, Wu Fang went out. That impersonation was astonishing. It would work; Carson was sure of it. But would it work if this man who was impersonating Kildare went directly to the governor general's office? The governor general hadn't met Kildare, and he might ask questions. On the other hand, Wu Fang probably knew what he was doing. The impersonator would go to the home of the American consul first and thence to the governor general.

The light that had illuminated the room faded as Wu Fang left. Carson stared up at the electric bulb in the socket directly over his head. He heard the rumble of the machinery as the panel closed behind Wu Fang, and the panel leading into the underground hanging garden was closing also.

Once more they were hemmed in and Wu Fang had told them their fate. Within an hour they would die. That electric bulb would go on when the electricity was turned on all over Singapore and they would be cooked, roasted like pigs. Singapore would suddenly become a city of a million and a half roasted human bodies.

Time passed, but Carson had no way of telling how long they remained there. All they could do was lie there and stare at each other. Carson could see the top of Kildare's head still resting on his leg but he couldn't see Kildare's face or eyes.

Suddenly, Carson became aware that the floor itself beside him was moving upward. A panel at the side of the room, one that had not been used as yet, was opening slowly with a whir of machinery, stopping a short distance above the floor. Something slithered through and the door closed again.

The figure that had crawled in stood up now. It was gigantic, and its forehead receded into a flat head. The face was ghastly and horrible to look upon. Zaru had returned and was moving across the floor ape fashion. He reached Tanya's side, muttering and cooing gently. Carson caught words out of that mumble— words in a garbled English.

"Tanya, you know me. Remember Zaru? Zaru, Tanya! They say Zaru crazy. Zaru love you from first time when you were little girl, when he kill your royal parents and steal you to bring to Wu Fang. Zaru watch for chance to save you, Tanya. You be mine! Mine, Tanya!"

With that, the beastly, cross-eyed figure straightened as he knelt on his knees beside Tanya. He thrust out his great chest and beat it with his fist like an enraged gorilla.

"You mine, Tanya!" he repeated. "Nobody take you away again. I know jungles where we hide forever. Apes know Zaru. Apes like Tanya when they know her. Zaru part ape."

The beast man stopped suddenly and stared down into the girl's face. Carson was struggling wildly to get free from that awful drug that held him but all of his struggles were mental, for he was still as paralyzed as the moment the needle had been pressed home in his neck.

There was no more evidence of the gas now; it had ceased shortly before Wu Fang had entered. Carson realized desperately that he must stop this beast-man. Still, Zaru said he was going to save Tanya. Perhaps—

Zaru was bending over the girl now and his enormous hands were stroking her cheek, caressing her white neck and shoulders. Carson got a glimpse of Tanya's eyes as Zaru moved out of his line of vision to stroke her arm. She was staring in awful fear and torment. Zaru sat back on his haunches now and began laughing.

"Tanya," he said. "I save you. Do not be afraid. Look what Zaru got."

Then out of that same pocket of his filthy robe, Zaru drew out a hypodermic needle, apparently the same one that he had used on Archibald Cameron.

"One push of the handle and you come all right," he crooned. "You will be able to move, Tanya. Then we go."

ZARU MOVED toward the girl's bare shoulder with the needle held in his right hand. Carson saw the needle prick the white, tender flesh of the lovely, blond girl, then that awful, stubby thumb of Zaru pressed the plunger. There was an instant of hesitation as Zaru turned back and drew out the needle, then Tanya moved, first her shoulder and then her arm. She sat up and jerked away from the beast man who was grinning at her greedily, but he reached out his hand and touched her.

The girl got to her feet and Zaru rose to stand beside her,

grinning. He reached out again and this time Tanya didn't shrink away as he touched her. Zaru was chuckling like a lunatic.

"Now you mine, Tanya," he said. "We go."

At that moment, Carson saw Tanya do something that to him was almost unbelievable. She put her soft white hand on the hairy neck of the beast man and moved it up to his flat, sunken cheek.

Her voice had a little tremble in it as she said, "Zaru, you have known me a long time. You were the one who killed my father and mother in order to steal me and bring me to Wu Fang. I just heard you say so. I do not hold that against you, yet you must admit that I have some rights. You must listen to me."

And now, to Carson's amazement, Tanya was standing directly in front of the hairy cross-eyed beast, stroking his flat forehead. It seemed to have a strange, calming effect on the beast.

"You know, Zaru," she said, "you can not escape Wu Fang. He is all powerful. I can not be yours unless Wu Fang is done away with."

The grin of anticipation on the face of Zaru faded suddenly. His tusked teeth gleamed in the weird light and his eyes dilated in an insane manner. Tanya turned and pointed to Carson and Kildare who were lying helpless on the floor.

"There," Tanya said, "is the solution, Zaru. If you will save these two men as well as me—if you will prick them with the needle—they will be able to get to Wu Fang and kill him."

Zaru pushed Tanya away from him. He seemed suddenly to be about to fly into a mad rage.

"No, no!" he cried. "That one there,"—he pointed directly at Carson—"you like him. You want me to save him for you. If I save him, you will go away with him. I take you now."

Zaru glanced at Tanya and then again at Carson. His ugly eyes gleamed and seemed more horribly crossed than ever.

"I kill him now," he said.

Suddenly Tanya threw both arms around Zaru, her left arm about his neck and her right arm under his shoulder.

"Zaru, listen to me," she cooed.

The girl's right hand was coming up, stroking Zaru's forehead again.

"Let us not waste time," Tanya said. "If you are going to take me away, let us go, but don't kill these two men. Wu Fang would be most angry. He will follow you and take me away from you if you deny him the supreme pleasure of killing Mr. Carson and Mr. Kildare. Hold me close, Zaru, for one moment, and then we will go."

Of all repulsive sights that Rod Carson had witnessed during his life, it seemed to him that this was the worst. When he saw Tanya clinging to the ape man and Zaru crushing her to him, it was almost more than he could stand.

Then suddenly, Tanya pushed Zaru away and said, "Now you lead the way. Open the panel and I will follow."

Carson realized now that Tanya held her right hand behind her. Zaru was grinning like a hungry beast. He nodded his flat head and turned abruptly toward the panels.

Instantly, Tanya whirled and without a sound, she dropped to Carson's side. The young explorer felt nothing for a moment but as Tanya rose again he could feel a warm glow rushing over him. He could move now, and could raise his head and his arms. He sat up as Tanya knelt beside Kildare.

Zaru turned from the panel wall just as the girl was rising from beside Kildare. The beast man's eyes flamed when he saw that the girl had tricked him. He lunged at her just as Carson managed to struggle to his feet.

Tanya fell back. Carson was up now, whipping out with lefts and rights as the beast man came at him, with clawed hands reaching for his throat. Then Kildare leaped at him, knocking him off balance so that the clutching hands barely missed Carson's throat.

Carson struck out with his left, which landed in the stomach of the hairy lunatic. It was as though his hand had struck a rock as it came into contact with those solid muscles. Again and again he struck.

Kildare lashed out with all his might. The power and strength of the great Zaru was almost unbelievable. Carson felt himself snatched up bodily and raised above Zaru's head. With a mighty effort Zaru hurled him at Kildare.

The government man caught Carson, but the terrific force sent them both crashing to the corner of the room. Dizzily, Carson tried to get up. He had a vision of Zaru leaping like a wild beast for Tanya. He snatched her by the arm and jerked her forward. Tanya let out a cry of pain.

"Zaru take you now," the hairy beast growled. "Not wait any more."

Carson struck out and kicked with all his might as Zaru

whirled. His shoe crashed into the bare ankle of the beast man and Zaru pitched forward. He caught himself, however, and leaped at the young explorer with a savage cry.

Carson and Kildare were up together. In desperation, Carson leaped at the madman like a panther. His hands caught the beast by the throat, and with all the strength he could muster, he pressed his thumbs home.

Zaru's right hand was thrown back and now it came swishing through the air in a blurred flash with the palm open. It struck Carson full in the jaw. His eyes danced and his head snapped to one side. As he went down, he saw Zaru spin around, swinging that powerful arm of his. He caught Kildare back of the ear with his knuckles and the government man was sent sprawling.

Both Kildare and Carson were on the floor. Carson was struggling to get up but he couldn't seem to make it. Zaru leaped across the floor and dragged Tanya with him toward the opening, like a caveman of old.

CHAPTER 15
THE CRIME LORD IN CHAINS

WITH TANYA under one arm, Zaru's hand shot to a panel. He dragged Tanya with him to the floor as, squealing and hissing, a horde of beasts rushed from the opening.

Zaru let out a half-animal scream of fear and pain. He let go of Tanya and the girl leaped away. The man-beast lay twitching on the floor, growing stiffer while the death beasts swarmed over him, sinking their fangs into every part of his flesh and tearing it from the bone.

"Get back!" Kildare cried, pushing Carson and Tanya to the opposite wall. "A club! Where's a club?"

He raised one foot to kick, but Tanya screamed, "No, no! I do not think it is necessary! Wait! I remember the location of the release button. It is there over that door. I saw Wu Fang touch it."

"But the beasts!" Carson cried, trying to hold Tanya back.

"Let me go, Rod, please," she begged. "The beasts will stay there with Zaru. I am sure of it."

Tanya broke loose from Carson's grasp and moved with lightning speed, never turning her course to dodge any of the beasts that swarmed over Zaru's body. Strangely enough, they seemed to pay no attention to her; their sole interest seemed to be in tearing Zaru apart as though there was something about the flesh of the man that drove them mad.

Carson reached out to stop Tanya, but he realized it was a perilous move, for if either of them fell they would be only a foot or so from the homed toads and the rat-headed lizards and the deadly snakes. The girl reached the panel, flung her hands up to the top of it and felt along the edge. Carson saw her press her finger down and then, as the whir of machinery came to them, she uttered a sob of triumph.

"I've got it!" she cried. "I've got it. We're free!"

The heavy panel was moving up rapidly, Tanya bent down and crept through.

"Come on!" she gasped. "Hurry!"

Carson plunged for the opening and Kildare pushed him ahead. Then that room was suddenly illuminated. There was nothing strange or weird about the light. It came from the single bulb that Wu Fang had screwed over their heads, and it glowed down innocently.

"The light is on!" Kildare cried. "Run for it! Any moment that killing circuit of electricity will be joined with this at the power house. Tanya, lead the way."

The three of them ran down the dark passage, Tanya leading, with Carson next and Kildare bringing up the rear.

The passage was almost pitch black, but with the same assurance that she had shown in leading Carson through some hours before, Tanya proceeded on her way.

"We do not go down this time!" she cried. "There is a secret way up. I think I can find it."

Tanya was panting. A moment later she cried out in warning to Carson, "Stop! You'll go over if you don't."

Carson tried to stop, but the floor was slippery and slimy with moisture, and he felt Kildare sliding up behind him. Desperately, he put out his arms to catch the rough walls to prevent himself from pushing Tanya over the brink.

"Get out of the way!" he cried. "I can't stop!"

Then, somehow, he and Kildare were wedged into the passage. There was a rending of clothing and Carson felt groping hands stopping him. Tanya was trying to hold fast to him.

"Rod," she gasped. "Hold me up. That's it! I've got to reach something."

Carson bent down, put his arms around Tanya's waist and lifted her up.

"There, that's it!" Carson heard her cry. "I've got it."

There came the grinding sound of one heavy stone rubbing against another.

"Now, up farther," Tanya said.

Carson lifted her as high as he could.

"There," she said. "Now take hold of my feet and push me the rest of the way. No, never mind. I have a toe hold in the wall. Come on, now, jump as high as you can and grab for a ledge in the darkness."

Carson leaped, and as his fingers clutched a ledge, he scrambled up with the toe of his shoe catching a hold in the rock wall. He turned and helped Kildare up.

There came that grinding sound again, and they found themselves in a narrow, stinking passage.

"Where does this take us?" Kildare asked as Tanya led them along the underground corridor. "It smells more like a sewer than an underground passage."

"It comes out on a street," Tanya told him. "Hold your nose. It will be easier. This passage we are in isn't used as a sewer, but the one adjoining it is. It's not very far, however."

They ran on, Carson and Kildare stumbling, but Tanya was as sure-footed as a cat.

"When we get out on the street," Kildare said, "we want to get to the nearest telephone."

"Yes," Tanya panted. "I was thinking of that. I know where there is one. We're almost there."

The stench was awful. Carson prided himself on having a stout stomach, but he found himself holding his nose with one hand as he ran.

Suddenly, Tanya cried, "Here we are." She gasped a little with surprise as she tried a door. "It's locked!" she cried.

Carson stepped forward, tried the latch.

"Yes, it's locked," he agreed. "It's quite solid, too. Step back, Tanya. I think Kildare and I can break it in."

The government man was feeling the door, groping down the sides. He turned around, put his back to Carson's and together they charged the door. It buckled, flung them back. They hurled at it again. There was a creak but the lock still hung. They tried it a third time.

Wham!

With a crashing sound, the door burst open. Carson and Kildare struggled to keep their balance as they plunged inward. An electric bulb burned on beyond, and they understood things better now. This was the wash room of a crude laundry. That was why this old sewer led there. It had been remodeled into an underground passage.

Carson stared at the single electric bulb that glowed at the other end of the room.

"Has that light got the—" he started to ask.

"It hasn't hurt us yet," Kildare cut in. "Come on."

THE GOVERNMENT man was leading the way now, beside Tanya. A Chinese face appeared around a door ahead and then the door suddenly slammed shut. They heard a bolt sliding shut.

"Have we got to crash that door too?" Kildare asked.

"No," Tanya said. "There's another this way."

They passed through another entrance and found themselves on a dark, narrow street. A lamp burned dimly at the corner.

"Wu Fang hasn't made contact yet," Kildare cried. "Come on. Where's that telephone?"

"In here," Tanya said. "There's an all night Chinese lunch room just a few doors away. I'm wire there's a telephone there."

"Good."

Kildare drove through the door of the Chinese lunch room. Tanya and Carson waited at the door and heard the proprietor of the shop say something to the government man. They saw Kildare's face darken as the bell jangled in the telephone. He picked up the receiver and called the operator. Then, as he waited, a strange, haggard look came over his face. Suddenly he slammed down the receiver on the hook.

"It's cut off," he said. "Any other telephone near here?"

"I hear no telephones in town work tonight," the Chinese proprietor said.

"Where did you hear that?" Kildare demanded.

"I have important call to make. Telephone here not work. I go next door. That no work. Go second door. Nobody's telephones work. Somebody say explosion at telephone company headquarters."

"What?" Kildare barked. "Good Lord!"

He burst out on the street again yelling, "Taxi! Taxi!"

But in that narrow, filth-drenched street there were no cabs. There was a car standing down at the corner, but no one was

The white men's revolvers echoed through the building.

in it. Kildare led them toward it, and without an instant's hesitation, he leaped into the front seat and started the motor. Tanya and Carson piled in beside him and the car roared off.

Somebody cried out from the front of a shop but they paid no attention.

There was a squeal of tires a few minutes later, as they drew up in front of the police headquarters that Sir Reginald Owen had so recently commanded. Kildare rushed inside past the startled police officers.

"I'm Val Kildare," he said hurriedly, "of the United States Secret Service. Sir Reginald Owen has been killed. He was hung by Wu Fang, and we have just escaped. Wu Fang is at the power house now. Turn off all your lights and order all lights in Singapore turned off. Come at once to the power house and be ready for a fight to the finish. We would like to have a couple of guns to take along, too."

The English inspector sitting at the desk nodded.

"Righto," he said. "We've been looting for Sir Reginald. We'll be on the job at once, sir. Thanks for tipping us off."

He handed a gun to Kildare and one to Carson. Both turned immediately and plunged out to the car again.

"Now, Tanya, do you know where the power house is?" Kildare asked.

Tanya nodded and they sped off. Four or five minutes passed, then suddenly, the street lights went off.

"Good," Kildare said. "That's something. If we can only get the house lights off now."

"But that's impossible," Carson interrupted. "They would

have to notify everyone in Singapore. The only way that we can be sure is to get to the central transformer stations and then—"

"Yes, I know," Kildare said. "It's hopeless. We've got to catch Wu Fang and his whole gang. We've got to get their machine, and their plans—everything."

Tanya was leaning forward in the center of the front seat, pointing straight ahead.

"See those big buildings down there with the stacks?" she said. "They hold the big generators and the steel turbines. I heard Wu Fang talking about them."

The car pulled up in front of the main building and Carson leaped out and stared about. Tanya started to follow him but he pushed her back gently.

"No, no!" he said. "Please hide in the back seat of the car until this is over."

Tanya hesitated. Kildare nodded his agreement.

"Yes, Tanya," he said. "That would be best. Wu Fang and his agents would give a lot to get you. Kneel down in the back seat of the car and stay there until we return." The government man whirled to Carson. "Come on, Rod!" he said.

At the entrance to the power house, they found the way blocked. Two slant-eyed yellow men leaped out in their path. At the same time they saw a light, just inside the door, shining down on the body of a night guard.

The arm of one yellow beast raised. There was an ugly knife in it that he was about to throw.

"Let him have it!" Kildare barked.

Blam!

Both Carson's and Kildare's guns boomed.

"Save your shots!" Kildare warned. "Come on!"

AS THE two men fell, Kildare and Carson lunged on over their bodies and went inside. They saw several things distinctly. On one side was a strange machine, apparently ancient and very crude. At that moment, Wu Fang himself was placing a belt from the wheel of one of the turbines to the drive wheel of the crude generating machine.

There was a strange light illuminating the place, but Carson saw that it was not shed by any electric bulbs. Instead, it was supplied by flares of some weird material that burned but gave off no smoke.

Wu Fang spun around and leaped behind the turbine as Carson and Kildare's revolvers bellowed and echoed through the great building. Bullets screamed as they struck the side of the turbine and ricocheted off.

There came the screaming command of Wu Fang's voice, then it seemed to Carson that the whole interior of the place erupted yelling, screaming, fighting savages of all descriptions. Now he saw that they came from a little iron balcony just over the entrance, leaping down to attack.

Carson was pulling his trigger as fast as he could, the commands of Wu Fang still ringing in his ears.

A black beast of a man grabbed him by the shoulder and spun him around. Carson saw a brutal fist upraised and coming down at him. His gun barked and the big black hulk swayed and toppled over.

His gun was empty and he was trying to fill it. Wu Fang was

the man that he must get. Carson leaped clear, shoving more bullets in his gun and trying to get around to the back of that great turbine.

Blam! Blam! Blam!

His gun was working again and yellow men and Malayans fell. Then suddenly, Carson remembered Tanya out there in the car. Would these men know that she was there? They must have seen her go out and get into the car again. He would have to get to that door.

A mass of humanity suddenly poured through the front door of the power office. They were the police of Singapore, and the place became a bedlam of shouts and shots.

Carson continued to wade through them as they came, fighting and tearing their way. Things became hazy, and then, as there was a sudden lull in the fighting, Carson became aware that someone was holding him up. Blood was trickling down his face from a cut over his eye.

Still he struggled; he must get to Tanya. Then he was being pushed out of the door with many others, and there was a rattling of chains and a clanking of handcuffs that mingled with the groaning of the wounded agents of Wu Fang.

Carson reached the car and looked inside. With a sickly feeling at the pit of his stomach, he realized that Tanya was not there. The car was empty!

"Tanya! Tanya!" he cried.

There was no answer. What could have happened to her?

Carson was still staring in amazement when men came up behind him. Englishmen, Chinese, and Malayans.

165

"That seems to clear the thing up," Carson heard Kildare say. "Well, at last, Wu Fang, we've got you."

Carson turned, as he heard the clanking of chains, and saw Wu Fang standing there, hands and feet tightly bound.

"We've got you this time," the Englishman in charge of the Singapore police was saying. "You've slipped out pretty cleverly before, but you won't make a get away now. We'll have you under guard constantly and you'll be chained to your cell."

"Everything is cleared up," Kildare was saying with a satisfied smile. "We've got the drawings of the apparatus and we've smashed the apparatus that they set up here. He didn't quite get it started in time to kill the residents of Singapore."

Carson heard all of those things through a sort of red haze that enveloped him. He blinked, gulped, and said in a voice that sounded far off, "But Tanya—she's gone. She was here in the car and—"

"It is written," Wu Fang cooed through his thin, cruel lips, "that defeat is often nearest when victory appears to have come."

POPULAR PUBLICATIONS
HERO PULPS

LOOK FOR MORE SOON!

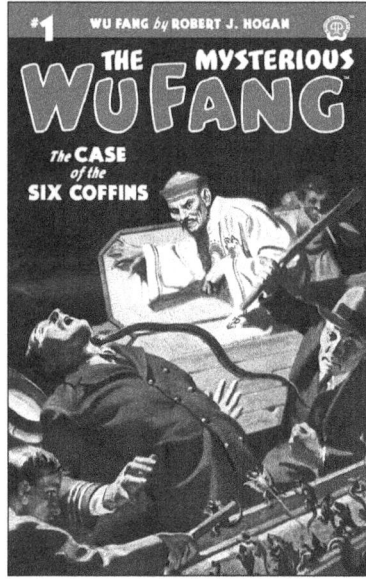